小樹系列

Little Trees

小樹系列

Little Trees

七片葉子

SEVEN LEAVES

涓滴水—撰 文

湯耀洋—英 譯

每個人心裡都該有座神仙花園

涓滴水

青少年時期，對很多人來說都是成長與蛻變的開始。生理與心理皆產生很劇烈的變化；看人、看事、看周遭都變得敏感而尖銳。要適應感受不一樣的環境，要重新認識開始陌生的自己。希望得到別人的肯定與認同，但又覺得朋友與家人總不瞭解自己。以為成熟強壯到可以應對任何事，但當遇到重大事件，卻發現自己其實很無力也很脆弱。

這也是當我接到幸惠師姊的邀約寫故事時，內心感到很惶恐的原因。

以我自己來說，那段青澀時期遇到相當多重大的人生考驗，包括生離與死別。用今日已事過境遷的心境來看，這段過程早就是歷經見山是山、見山疑是山、見山不是山、見山又是山的輕鬆自在；但對那個少年十五二十時的孩子來講，情感路上高低起伏、崎嶇難行，要能自在承受與好好面對，真的很不容易。

林幸惠師姊不只是位好作家，也是一位懂心理學的屬害說客。她用「同理心」這個強大的字眼，娓娓道來自己的初發心，說著她對於努力尋找答案的孩子們之感動與心疼。當孩子面臨溝通的過程與猶豫不決時，故事設定天界的綠葉仙子翩然降臨人間、來到了眼前，並以聰慧而超然的觀點提供了意見。

然後，有了後續每個星期跟一個孩子的心靈密集相處時間，一一探索他們心中深層的恐懼、疑問、祕密、渴望與迷惑。同時小綠仙子也開啟了我的視野與想像力，引領我發掘孩子們原本就具有的善良、敏銳、勇敢、自信、決斷力；一同換個角度與立場來思考問題，釋放正能量、發揮能力解決困惑。

聽著丁曉雨說著面對誘惑難以決定的兩難，跟著一起擔心與傷腦筋。

看到王子強迷失自我、找不到存在價值的過程，著急也心疼。

方雅蘋一心想當網紅，面對幻滅受到打擊的難過，很想拍拍她的肩膀，告訴她優秀的表現方式有很多種，路永遠不只一條。

謝佑青用以牙還牙的方式來逃避真正的需求，真想讓他早點發現與面對。

吳欣潔的心病與傷痛讓人難過，也不由自主流了許多眼淚。

　　郭彥志那一巴掌的疼，同樣也感同身受他失去目標的自我放逐。

　　許佳綺對面子與友情的錯誤解讀，真想狠狠責備一番、用力勸醒她。

　　看到他們由困惑與自我懷疑中走出來，真切感到療癒與欣慰。一如慶幸好朋友遇上人生難題時，能做出不錯的抉擇。

　　青少年時期，有太多年輕的孩子在自己的世界裡努力振翅，想要學飛、想要冒險、想要探索更廣大更寬闊的世界。心疼他們在這個階段，遇到生命中的各種難題與問題，辛苦地在原地打轉或茫茫然找不到答案。真心冀望《七片葉子》能提供他們一些參考建議與方向指引。

　　《七片葉子》是一個關於仙女與魔法的奇幻故事，也是一個關於愛的成長與學習故事；期許這本書像一面鏡子，讓讀者也能看到自己人生的轉機，得到調適與修補的機會。

　　希望每個人的心中都能有座神仙花園，有讓人驚豔的奇花異草、雄偉的參天大樹、更有取之不盡的奇幻妙葉。

當境遇一來，自己心中的靈透仙子翩然到來，成為最強大的後盾，指引自己走出困境，積極改變命運。

涓滴之水、匯成江河。最後想跟親愛的讀者們分享，人的一生有無數的一點一滴，看似微不足道，但累積下來回頭看，不論酸甜苦辣鹹各種滋味，都是歷練與能量，也都會是好風景。

希望我們多關注周圍年輕的孩子，及時伸出援手，一起成為守護他們的好心仙子群。

contents

目錄

Mission One   At the crossroads

第一個任務
Mission One

十字路口的選擇
At the crossroads

"I must go? I mustn't go?"
"Should I go? Shouldn't I go?"
"Yes, I can go? No, I can't go?"

As Ding Xiao-yu walked down the street, her mind was on these questions rather than on the roads and traffic. She thought that she had been offered a super easy job. What could possibly be wrong with that job? Would there be a catch? Considering the pay, taking it should have been an easy decision to make, but somehow she just couldn't make up her mind.

"Watch out!", "Dangerous!", "Watch where you're going!" Screaming people, honking cars, and screeching brakes dragged Ding out of her deep thoughts and back to reality. But before she could make sense of those noises, in midair in front of her a pair of hands popped up, one of which grabbed Ding's arm firmly so that she couldn't take another step forward into the lane of moving cars and the other hand gently patted her shoulder. She heard a sweet voice saying "Ding Xiao-yu, the roads are a hazardous place. Watch your every step and don't be distracted."

「去？還是不去？」
「去？還是不該去？」
「去？還是不能去？」

丁曉雨走在路上，腦海裡浮現的全是一個個的問號。她心想：不過是個輕鬆打工賺錢的機會，沒那麼嚴重吧？可是不知道為什麼，就是遲遲無法做決定！

「小心！」「危險！」「走路不看路啊！」就在自己陷入決定的兩難時，四周響起了尖銳的喇叭聲、煞車聲、尖叫聲！
突然騰空冒出一雙手，真的是騰空，丁曉雨瞪大雙眼，緊盯著那雙不知從哪裡冒出來的手；其中一隻手緊緊地拉著自己的手臂，阻止了丁曉雨差點衝到馬路中的腳步；另一隻手輕拍自己的肩膀，清脆甜美的聲音響起。
「丁同學，馬路如虎口，每一步都要小心，要專心。」

Ding Xiao-yu looked around. Everything seemed to have slowed down to stillness, moving only in double slow motion or as fast as a turtle.

"Hello, I'm Green Fairy. Just call me GF," said the owner of the mysterious hands that had just saved her from a chaos. Ding saw a friendly smile.

Ding took a quick glance at GF but couldn't resist the curiosity to size her up.

GF wore short hair with fine braids on top that served as a headband. Her face was smooth like flawless light-pink porcelain with a touch of red, making her eyes brighter and livelier. She might as well be a classical beauty walking off an ancient painting. Made of either silk or cotton fabric of the highest grade, her clothes, in all shades of green, fitted her just right. Her finely proportioned physique moved with elegance. She did appear a bit "out of this world", literally or figuratively.

丁曉雨看著四周景象，覺得好奇怪，四周所有的人好像同時約好放慢了速度，以接近定格的狀態存在，包括路口等紅燈準備過馬路的學生、上班族、以及剛剛差點撞上自己的紅色轎車；連平常呼嘯而過的汽車與摩托車也是以龜速前進。

「妳好！我是綠葉仙子，叫我小綠就好！」騰空出現的雙手原來有一個笑容很親切的主人。

丁曉雨急促的瞧了一眼，又忍不住好奇地上下打量。

笑容的主人留著俏麗的學生頭短髮，頭上還有像髮箍般的細緻編髮；臉的皮膚像白瓷一般無瑕且粉裡透紅，襯得聰慧的大眼更加靈活晶亮；五官細緻得像古畫裡走出來的古典美人；身上的衣服有著深深淺淺濃濃淡淡的綠，材質不知是絲綢還是最高等級的棉麻，合身中帶點飄逸的氣質；身形修長、動作優雅、是帶著點仙氣。

"I skipped breakfast this morning. It must have caused me to be anemic and unable to see clearly," Ding Xiao-yu said to herself, rubbing her eyes and not believing what she was seeing.

"I am in charge of gardens and grounds in heaven, where I work happily every day. One day, many seeds sprouted in the seedling area. That sight delighted me, and while enjoying the moment, I stepped on and crushed seven sprouts. As a punishment, I was sent to this temporal world to accomplish seven missions: to help seven children who emit distress signals for help." GF's voice was very pleasing, but Ding couldn't make sense of what she was saying.

"I'll never skip breakfast again! I'm seeing this strange being in broad daylight? Perhaps she is a fairy?" Ding Xiao-yu mumbled to herself and shook her head.

"Ding Xiao-yu, you're my first mission," declared Green Fairy earnestly.

「我一定是因為偷懶沒吃早餐，所以貧血眼花了！」丁曉雨揉揉眼睛，不敢相信。

「我負責天界的園藝，每天都快樂歡喜地工作。有一天看到我照顧的幼苗區好多幼苗都發芽成長了，因為太開心、太得意，一個不小心踩壞了七株幼苗，所以被罰來到凡間完成七個任務，幫助七個發出求救訊號的孩子。」小綠的聲音很好聽，但丁曉雨實在沒辦法聽懂她所講的話。

「以後我絕對不敢不吃早餐了！居然大白天看到奇怪的人？或者是仙子？」丁曉雨搖頭晃腦，喃喃自語。

「丁曉雨同學，妳是我的第一個任務。」小綠認真的宣布。

"My mission is to give you this mysterious present and teach you how to use it to solve your problems," GF continued. Suddenly, an elongated cloth bag popped up in her hand, the one that had grabbed Ding moments before. She carefully gave the bag to Ding Xiao-yu.

"Present?" Ding Xiao-yu was confused, but she thought this GF who had just saved her from an accident should be a good person or a kind-hearted fairy.

"There are two things in the bag: an incense stick from heaven and a divine leaf," Green Fairy said gently. "When the moon comes up, light the incense stick and look at the veins of the leaf attentively. Then allow your mind to follow the veins, and the answer to your question will show up."

Ding Xiao-yu hesitated a little but still accepted the gift.

"An answer to my problem? I myself can't even solve my issue; what can an incense stick and a leaf possibly tell me?"

「我的任務就是要送妳這個神祕禮物！並且教妳如何使用，幫助妳解決問題。」自稱小綠的女生長相很清秀，她伸出剛剛拉住丁曉雨的手，手掌上忽然出現一個細長型的布包，很慎重地交給丁曉雨。

「禮物？」丁曉雨覺得有點莫名其妙，但這位小綠剛剛才救了自己，避免了一場意外車禍，應該是個好人或好心的仙子吧！

「這份禮物有兩樣東西，一支天香加一片仙葉。」小綠溫柔地說明。「晚上等月亮出來的時候，妳點這支天香，然後專心地看著這片葉子上的紋路，接著讓妳的心念跟著葉脈走，心中的問題就會出現答案。」

丁曉雨有點遲疑，接下了禮物。

「答案？我自己都找不到答案，一支香跟一片葉子能告訴我什麼？」

"The divine incense stick is awesome. It's like a high-speed Wi-Fi transceiver between the temporal world and heaven," GF said. "Haven't you heard the expression that a fallen leaf presages the arrival of autumn? A little clue can lead to big developments, so don't underestimate this leaf, which is like you human being's MR, or mixed reality."

Ding Xiao-yu was still very befuddled.

"The answer? You'll find it," Green Fairy said, smiling. Then she vanished as suddenly as she had appeared. Everything returned to normal speed. Automobiles sped by and hustle and bustle abounded all around Ding.

Ding Xiao-yu couldn't take her mind off her questions and the answer that Green Fairy had promised.

"Dad has a hard job that doesn't pay very much. Mom is extremely thrifty, pinching every penny. Every time I want to buy a book or daily necessities or ask for an allowance, she gives me an earful," Ding Xiao-yu said to herself, quite upset by the gloomy picture. "I wish I could grow up fast and begin to make money for myself. Then I can buy whatever I want without asking Mom for money."

「天香很厲害的，就像是人間跟天界的 Wi-Fi 高速通訊接收器。」「妳沒聽過一葉知秋嗎？小跡象也可以看到大發展的。千萬別小看這片葉子，葉子就像妳們人間的 MR，也就是立體混合實境。」

丁曉雨的表情還是非常疑惑。

「答案啊，妳會知道的！」小綠笑笑，就像她忽然出現一樣，又忽然消失；四周又恢復了車水馬龍，人聲車聲再度響起。

丁曉雨一整天都沉浸在自己的煩惱中。

「爸爸賺錢不多、工作也辛苦；媽媽平常很節省、用錢很計較。自己每次開口買書、買日用品、要零用錢都會被碎碎唸。」丁曉雨很懊惱。「我真想快點長大，有能力賺錢，想買什麼就買什麼，不用看家人的臉色。」

Little Cai, a cousin of Ding's classmate, knew about Ding's desire to make money. He also thought Ding should work. Yesterday he told Ding about an easy job with great pay.

"You just need to call and chat with a few people. Super easy! You have a sweet voice and you're convincing. You'll be a great fit for the job."

"Don't you love to buy handbags and clothes? Your mom and dad are very strict with you, and they tell you that you can't buy this and that. That's very unreasonable. And your allowance is pathetic. How can that possibly be enough?" Little Cai said.

"This job pays really well for your effort. You look smart and you're quick-witted. That's why I told you about this great job. I don't just tell everyone about it, you know," Little Cai continued.

"It's really not hard at all, and we have a script, which you can just read out loud on your calls. Don't worry. We have prepared a list of responses that you can use to handle every reaction and every objection from the people you are calling. Their reactions to your call just can't trip you up. It's as simple as that," Little Cai persisted in his argument.

同學的表哥小蔡知道自己的想法，也表示認同。昨天他還熱心介紹輕鬆打工賺錢的方法，簡單就能領高薪。

「只需要跟幾個人打打電話，聊聊天而已，超簡單！妳的聲音很好聽，也很有說服力，非常適合。」

「妳不是喜歡買包包買衣服嗎？妳爸媽常常管東管西，限制妳買東西，很不合理欸，妳零用錢那麼少，哪裡夠用啊！」

「這個打工真的很好賺，妳看起來很聰明，反應也很快！我才報這個好康給妳。我可不是什麼人都說的！」

「真的不難！我們都有現成寫好的腳本，妳只要照著唸就好。妳放心！各種反應、各種問題我們都有事先找好答案，不會被考倒的！就是這麼簡單！」

"Let's do this. If you're still worried, let me add you to my FB, where you can see my sidekicks...er, no, my employees and the messages and photos that they've shared. I guarantee that you'll envy them a whole lot," Little Cai kept on talking.

And he went on talking, "Go to FB to see for yourself, and then you'll know everything I say is true. My employees all live in luxurious rental homes; they own many, many brand-name handbags; they often eat at fancy restaurants and drive fancy cars. And they have more money than they know what to do with."

"After you've watched it, you'll blame me for not telling you about it sooner," Little Cai said.

"I'm not kidding; you really can earn enough very quickly to buy luxurious goods and satisfy your every desire," Little Cai concluded with an exaggerated expression.

Still Ding Xiao-yu was only half believing. She worried that there would be no such thing as a free lunch under the sun.

「這樣好了，如果妳還是擔心，我臉書加妳好友，妳去看看我的跟班們……喔，不！我的其他員工們，他們臉書分享的訊息跟照片，包妳一定羨慕死！」

「妳去臉書自己看看就知道我説的都是真的，我那些屬下都是住豪宅，擁有好多名牌包跟漂亮衣服、常常吃各種好吃的大餐、開好車、還有用不完的鈔票！」

「嘖嘖嘖，看了之後妳會怪我的！怪我這麼慢才告訴妳！」

小蔡誇張的表情強調著：「真的很快就能賺錢買奢侈品哦，可以滿足各種慾望呢。」

可是丁曉雨還是半信半疑，擔心天下沒有白吃的午餐。

During a recess, she went to the library to check it out on FB. She saw those people showing off their riches. Ding was envious and worried all at once.

"I must go? I mustn't go?"
"Should I go? Shouldn't I go?"
"Yes, I can go? No, I can't go?..."
"Are there really no strings attached? Is it as easy as Little Cai said?"
"Is this really a lucky break for me? Won't it be a poison beautifully sugar coated?"
"How should I choose?"
"What decision should I make?"
The more Ding Xiao-yu tried to reach an answer, the more questions she raised.

That night at home after finishing homework, Ding Xiao-yu took out the mysterious present that she had received from Green Fairy on the way to school that morning. She curiously opened the cloth bag and saw a slender incense stick showing two printed characters, but they were too blurry to make out. A fresh, green leaf was also in the bag. It looked not much different from any other leaf, but it did give off a light aroma that's quite pleasant.

她趁下課時到圖書館查了一下臉書。看著那些炫富照，心裡又是羨慕又是擔心。

「去？還是不去？」
「去？還是不該去？」
「去？還是不能去？」
「真的沒有問題？這麼輕鬆簡單？」
「真的是難得的幸運好機會？會不會是危險的糖衣毒藥？」
「究竟應該怎麼選擇？」
「該做什麼決定呢？」
問號不但沒有消失，反而越來越多了。

到了晚上，做完功課，丁曉雨拿出了今天上學收到的神祕禮物，好奇地打開研究。布包裡放著一支細細長長的香，上面隱隱地浮現著兩個字，可惜模模糊糊地看不太清楚。還有一片鮮活的綠色葉片，跟一般葉子好像沒什麼不同，只是散發著淡淡清香，聞起來很舒服。

"All right, now I'm safely at home, so it won't hurt to give it a try." Ding Xiao-yu said.

She carefully lit the incense stick. Slowly, smoke went up without being disturbed by any breeze.

Golden light slowly flowed into the leaf on the table. Quickly, the golden light spread to every vein of the tree.

The cloth bag evaporated into thin air without a trace or a sound.

Ding Xiao-yu looked at the leaf attentively. Without her knowing it, her mind was already following the veins, and she felt that the leaf was getting bigger and bigger. Before long she was walking on a golden path. She saw mountains, streams, and high-rise buildings in the distance. The scene appeared real and virtual in equal proportion. Suddenly thin, transparent screens popped up in front of her, each showing some sound and color video.

The first to show up were the people that Ding had seen showing off their wealth on FB, but now she could hear conversations and saw motions.

「好吧！我在家裡應該很安全，試一下應該沒有關係。」

丁曉雨小心翼翼地點燃了天香，沒有風，煙裊裊地向上飄動著。

桌上的那片葉子緩緩地像被注入了金黃色的流光，金絲般的光線迅速地流過每一條細細的葉脈與紋路。

布包由固體變成氣體，無聲無息地消失在空氣當中。

丁曉雨專心地研究著葉子，讓思緒不知不覺跟著葉脈走動，漸漸感覺葉子越變越大，自己竟然在一條金色大道上漫步，遠處有山有水也有高樓大廈，只是景象真實中帶點虛擬。眼前忽然浮現一個個透明的薄幕，上面閃動著彩色的聲光與畫面。

首先出現的，是在臉書上看到的那些炫富照。不同的，是現在有了聲音對白與動作。

"Why toil to make just a few bucks? These days nothing can make you money faster than fraud." said one of those people.

"In ancient times, people robbed the rich to help the poor, but we aren't picky. Whoever has money is our prey. Haha," said another.

"Those fools are so easy to scam. Just say a few sentences in an indistinct voice to those fools and they'll believe that their son or daughter was kidnapped and given a beating; or they will believe that their long-lost friends badly need money from them. It's amazing how many fools will fall for such nonsense talk."

"Use people's greed to deceive them. For example, tell them that they have won the lottery and congratulations, but first they must pay taxes. Oodles of fools have fallen for that scheme. It's just too easy."

"Unbelievable. People just don't check before they act. Just tell them that their online credit card payment was made in error. Their one charge was mistakenly charged as installment payments, making their total charge many times more than the correct amount," yet another person on the screen said. "Then tell them to go to an ATM and follow my instructions to get the money credited back to their account. It just amazed me how many fools had done as I told them to."

「哈！幹嘛努力賺錢啊！這年頭用騙的賺最快！」

「人家古時候是劫富濟貧，我們不挑，誰身上有錢我們就騙誰！嘻！」

「那些傻瓜笨蛋真好騙，裝幾句聽不清楚的聲音說是他們的兒子或女兒被打、被綁架，或是好久沒聯絡的朋友急需用錢，這麼瞎的設計也可以騙倒一堆人！」

「利用貪心這一點也可以騙不少人，像說：你中獎了！恭喜恭喜！請先轉帳繳稅金，也可以讓一堆人上當！哈！太簡單了！」

「笑死人了，都不求證的！跟他們說刷卡線上付款刷錯了，整筆刷成分期，帳單金額變成很多倍，讓他們去提款機跟著操作就可以退錢回帳戶，這麼蠢的腳本竟然那些呆子們也會照著做！」

"Some of us were even worse. They told the fool that his credit cards, ID card, and national health insurance card were stolen or impounded and his accounts were frozen. They told him to transfer money to get back their things. Some fools really did send money over. Some of them, unwittingly, called the numbers we had supplied to them to report their case and made appointments with our fake police and fake prosecutor to hand money over to our guys."

"Those fools were so clueless that they deserved to be scammed. If they're willing to fork over their money, we certainly should spend it."

"If they don't know better, they should at least have some common sense. If they don't have common sense, at least they should watch TV to know about the fraudulent schemes that scammers used to cheat people out of their money. I love to dupe the fools who don't have common sense and don't watch TV. They are the easiest to defraud."

"Haha, I'm so thrilled. Who cares if the fools lost their shirt."

Ding Xiao-yu watched them sitting on piles of money to show off their schemes and their wealth without shame much less compunction. Suddenly Ding felt that the luxurious goods were not quite so attractive as before, and she began to sense some uneasiness.

「還有更狠的！騙他們說信用卡、健保卡、身分證被偷被扣住，說帳戶被凍結不能使用，要他們付錢轉帳來贖，也有人呆呆轉帳進來。還有人照我們給的假電話報案報資料，跟我們安排的假警察、檢察官碰面繳錢。」

「活該被騙嘛！錢送上門來讓我們用，當然要用！」

「沒有知識也要有常識，沒常識就要常看電視！我最喜歡這些沒知識、沒常識又不看電視的人了！真好騙！」

「哈哈哈！太開心了！誰管他們死活啊！」

丁曉雨看著坐在錢堆裡口沫橫飛、囂張炫富、那幾張扭曲不屑的嘴臉，突然覺得那些奢侈品沒那麼吸引人了，心裡也開始覺得有點不舒服。

"Do I really, truly want to be part of these grifters?" Ding Xiao-yu asked herself.

When Ding Xiao-yu's attention returned to the complex veins of the leaf, her mind took her down another vein. On the golden path in front of her was a silver-haired elderly woman. She dressed neatly but appeared a little flustered. Her wrinkled hands were trembling, and she couldn't stop wiping her tears.

"I don't want to drag down my son and his family. They are all good people. The bad guys can't just impound their bank accounts where my son and his wife keep their hard-earned money. My son is a public servant and my daughter-in-law is a teacher. Their two sons are so lovely. I shouldn't drag them down simply because some cons have hijacked my bank account," the elderly woman said.

Worries and anxiety were written all over the face of the elderly woman, her voice sounding a little like sobbing. Though she looked very nervous and her hair was a little messy, she still looked dignified, elegant, and genteel.

她猶疑地問自己。「我真的……真心想成為他們之間的一分子嗎？」

丁曉雨回過神，再度看著錯綜複雜的葉脈，思緒朝著另一條紋路方向移動。眼前金色大道上出現了一個衣服整齊、神色有點慌張的銀髮老太太。她滿是皺紋的手一直顫抖著，還不停地擦著眼角的淚水。

「我不想連累我的兒子跟媳婦一家人啊，他們都是老老實實的好人，不能查扣他們的帳戶啊，他們都是辛辛苦苦賺錢的。我兒子是公務員，我媳婦是老師，兩個孫子都很可愛，不能因為我的帳戶被盜用就連累他們啊！」

老婦人的焦急完全顯露在臉上，聲音帶點哭腔。她氣質端莊優雅，雖然現在看起來很緊張失常，頭髮也有點亂，但是風度還是很好。

"How much money did you say needed to be transferred? I have another account that is just for my pension. I was going to use it when I am older. If I get sick, I don't want to be a burden to my son and his family. If there is money left after I die, it can be my grandsons' college funds," the old woman said.

"Please, don't impound the accounts of my son and my daughter-in-law. I haven't ever wronged anybody in my life, and I haven't ever done bad things. I didn't mean for my account to be hijacked. Okay, I'll use my retirement fund to pay the security deposit so long as you leave my son and his family alone." the elderly woman pleaded.

"How much is the penalty and security deposit? What? That much? Then I'll have very little left in my pension account. You'll return the security deposit to me, right? Right? You really will?"

"Okay, tell me the time and place. I'll be right over." she continued.

The elderly woman held on tightly to her purse as she walked away—slowly, alone, stooped.

「你説應該轉多少錢過去？我還有另一個帳戶是放我的退休金的，是我留著養老用的，如果我生病不想連累我兒子他們，將來萬一有剩也可以當我兩個孫子的學費預備金。」

「千萬不要去查扣我兒子跟媳婦的帳戶啊，我一輩子沒害過人，我真的沒做過壞事啊，帳戶被盜用真的不是我故意的，我拿我的退休老本繳罰金跟保證金好了，只要不害到我兒子他們就好。」

「你們説要繳多少罰金跟保證金？什麼？要這麼多錢啊！那我的退休金剩下就不多了，保證金會還我吧！會嗎？真的會嗎？」

「好！告訴我地點跟時間，我馬上過去。」

老太太緊抓著錢包，孤單佝僂的背影漸漸蹣跚離去，滿頭銀白的頭髮遠遠地顫動著。

An indescribable feeling overwhelmed Ding Xiao-yu that made her shout to the old woman, "Don't go! Don't you go there. Those are a whole bunch of swindlers out to scam you."

But that old woman just disappeared from Ding's sight. A nervous-looking middle-aged man then appeared on the golden path. He anxiously rubbed his hands and paced back and forth. He looked worried and scared.

"Don't cry and don't be afraid. Daddy will figure out a way to protect you." he said.

"Please, please let my daughter go. She's young and inexperienced. She might have said things that rubbed you the wrong way. I apologize for her. She might have spoken too sharply but she is a kind-hearted person. You must have mistaken her for somebody else. She doesn't borrow money or fight against anybody. Please."

"I'm a single father. I have raised her all her life. She is very nice. I work overtime so that she may have a normal life like others. I don't want her to live worse than others simply because she has a single parent. How much does she owe you? I will pay you back, but please let her go."

有一種說不出的感覺從內心泉湧而上，丁曉雨急忙衝口而出：「不要去！不要去呀！那是詐騙集團騙你的！」

眼前的老太太消失了！金色大道緊接著出現一個緊張的中年男子，兩手焦慮地搓著，兩腳也不停踱步，臉上的神情又擔心又害怕。

「不要哭不要怕，爸爸會想辦法、爸爸會保護妳的。」

「拜託拜託，請你們放了我的女兒。她年輕不懂事，說錯話惹毛了你們，我替她跟你們道歉。她只是講話急，心腸很好的，你們一定是弄錯人了！她不會亂借錢或跟人打架吵架的，拜託你們了！」

「我是個單親爸爸。從小照顧她，看著她長大，她很乖的！我辛苦工作加班都是為了讓她能跟別人過一樣的生活，不會因為是單親家庭，就過著比人家差的苦日子。她欠你們多少錢，我來付，你們先放了她。」

"Three hundred thousand dollars? That much? I don't even have that much in my bank account. What can I do? Please don't beat her. Give me time to gather the money," the man grabbed his own hair and pleaded in a low voice. Anyone could tell that he was deeply troubled.

"Who will loan me money? The boss? Co-workers? Banks? Too slow. What am I to do? What am I to do?"

Ding Xiao-yu thought of her own father working and sweating under the hot sun as a construction worker. She bitterly shook her head and said in a low voice, "They're swindlers; they are cons. Don't fall into their trap."

But the middle-aged man had already vanished. Abruptly, those luxurious things and piles of money, far from attracting her, were making her feel like disgorging. Her stomach churned, her heart heavy.

Not far in front of her on the golden path, a figure walked toward her. It was Green Fairy.

"Hi, Ding Xiao-yu. Remember me? I'm GF. Have you found the answer?" GF said.

「三十萬？這麼多！我銀行沒這麼多錢，怎麼辦？你們不要打她，拜託拜託，給我時間去籌錢。」

中年男子抓著頭髮低聲懇求，看得出來非常苦惱。

「我可以跟誰借錢？跟老闆預支？跟同事借？還是跟銀行借信貸？太慢了！怎麼辦？怎麼辦？」

想起自己當建築工的爸爸在烈日下揮汗工作的模樣，丁曉雨有點苦澀地搖頭，輕聲地說：「是騙子，他們是騙子啊！不要上當！」

中年男子也消失了！丁曉雨忽然覺得那些奢侈品與鈔票散發著讓人作嘔的味道，胃在翻攪、心也很沉重。

金色大道的前方不遠處，今天馬路上拉了一把救了自己的小綠迎面走來。

「丁曉雨同學，記得我嗎？我是小綠。妳找到答案了嗎？」

In reply, Ding Xiao-yu, a little lost, shook her head at first, but then nodded.

GF smiled and looked at Ding meaningfully.

"Do you know that you almost went down the wrong path? Lucky for you, it's not too late." GF said, waving her fingers slightly. A screen quickly moved toward them from far in the back.

"You almost went there." GF said as she pointed at the screen.

On the screen, sirens blared as police cars sped near. Officers broke into a big house and dragged out some people whom Ding Xiao-yu had seen on Little Cai's FB — where they proudly showed off their wealth. But now, they hung their heads, walking out of their ill-gotten property in shame, and trying to hide their faces from reporters and their cameras.

A news anchor announced, "Yesterday the police stormed a multi-story building where a scam group headed by Little Cai was running its call center. The police arrested eight men and five women suspects and secured evidence. Since the suspects may flee, destroy evidence, or communicate with each other to device a defense, the prosecutors have petitioned the court to lock the crooks up without bail."

丁曉雨有點失神，微微地搖了搖頭又輕輕點了點頭。

小綠露出燦爛的微笑，意味深長地看著丁曉雨。

「妳知道嗎？妳差點走錯了路，做了錯誤的選擇！還好，現在還來得及！」小綠手輕輕一指，遠方薄幕浮現的畫面迅速逼近。

「這差一點是未來的妳。」

畫面裡，警車鳴笛聲由遠而近刺耳地響著，一群警察衝進炫富照裡的豪宅。那幾張曾經意氣風發、高談闊論的臉孔，瞬間變得垂頭喪氣、羞慚愧疚，低著頭不敢面對攝影鏡頭。

新聞主播的聲音響亮地播報著：「警調單位傍晚攻堅獨棟透天厝，破獲蔡姓主嫌為首的詐騙機房，當場查獲涉嫌 8 男 5 女共 13 名成員，以及查扣相關證物，並因有逃亡、湮滅證據和串供之虞而聲請拘押。」

Ding Xiao-yu saw Little Cai among the arrested. She seemed to also see a woman suspect who looked like Ding Xiao-yu. Ding stared at the screen again and realized that the woman was someone else.

GF said seriously to Ding, "Their fraudulent deeds were found out and they were arrested. One wrong step in the beginning has led to a series of wrong steps. It's not easy that you turned around and avoided taking that first wrong step just in time."

Ding Xiao-yu was glad that she hadn't been cheated by Little Cai and she was touched by Green Fairy, "GF, thanks a lot for your gift. Will we see each other again? "

Green Fairy smiled and looked at Ding, "Xiao-yu, I've accomplished my first mission, and I don't think we'll meet again," GF said.

"The leaf came from heaven, so it will begin to wither momentarily. All this will remain only in your memory," GF continued. "And the incense stick is about to finish burning. Take a look at the words on it. Those words are for you and you alone."

丁曉雨看到了小蔡，恍惚間她也似乎看到了很像自己的身影，再仔細專心盯著看，卻發現原來是看錯人。

小綠嚴肅認真地感嘆：「他們終究因為東窗事發被抓了。一步錯步步錯，及時回頭很不容易。」

丁曉雨心頭有著慶幸也有點感動，她忍不住開口問：「小綠，謝謝妳的禮物，我們還有機會再見嗎？」

小綠看著丁曉雨笑了笑，然後一句一句小聲地叮嚀：「丁曉雨同學，我的第一個任務已經完成，我們應該不會再見面了。」

「葉子來自天界，等下就會開始枯萎乾掉；一切的一切，只會留在妳的記憶當中。」
「天香快燒完了，妳趕快看一下天香留給妳的字，那是專屬於妳的訊息。」

Green Fairy gradually became lighter and lighter. She was almost transparent before vanishing altogether.

Ding Xiao-yu uttered in a hurry, "I'll remember you, GF. Thank you."

Ding turned to the incense stick, which had finished burning. All that was left was ash, which showed vague but discernible characters: No greed. The golden light in the veins of the divine leaf had completely disappeared, leaving only faint brown light.

GF had disappeared, but her voice echoed in Ding's room, "Ding Xiao-yu, you made an intelligent choice. Greed destroys its owners. A person wise enough to decline the temptation of greed is blessed. Congratulations!"

小綠的影子慢慢越來越淡，變得越來越透明。

丁曉雨趕緊說出：「我會記得妳的。小綠，謝謝妳。」

她回頭看向天香，天香已燃燒殆盡。灰燼裡若隱若現出現兩個字：不貪。葉脈上的金光已全部消失，四周只留下微弱暈黃的燈光。

小綠的影像消失了，但她的聲音在房間裡迴盪：「丁曉雨，妳做出了有智慧的選擇，貪念會毀了一個人，但是有智慧拒絕誘惑的人真的很讚。恭喜妳！」

Mission Two Be myself, but how?

第二個任務
Mission Two

當自己好辛苦
Be myself, but how?

After the school let out, Wang Zi-qiang walked slowly home. He had to hunch because his huge book bag was stuffed with textbooks, quizzes, study aids, and simulated tests for all subjects. Looking from a distance, he was like a turtle with a very large shell inching forward ever so slowly.

"Why did you get that question wrong on your monthly math quiz?"

"Why were you so careless? Couldn't you have double checked a few more times?"

"Is it really that tough for you to move up one place in your class standing?"

"You'd have gotten a perfect score if you had gotten this question right. What a pity."

"Never let up your effort. Always be high-strung. You must work hard to succeed."

As he dragged his feet inching toward home, the nagging of his mother played back in his head. When his mother was nagging, his father would largely be a silent observer, only occasionally giving him seemingly scolding glances. The thought of his mom and dad made his book bag, his steps, and his heart heavier as he got nearer to his home.

放學的時候，王子強弓腰駝背慢慢地走著；揹著裝滿了各科書籍、考卷與參考書、測驗卷的書包，遠遠看去就像是一隻背著沉重大殼的烏龜，緩慢爬行。

「為什麼月考數學還會錯一題？」
「你怎麼這麼粗心？難道不能多檢查幾次嗎？」
「要你進步一名有這麼難嗎？」
「就差這題你就滿分了！太可惜了！」
「不可以放鬆，隨時要繃緊，一定要努力才會成功！」

他心裡想著媽媽的那些叮嚀與叨唸，想著爸爸不說話也像是在責備的眼神，腳步越來越沉重。

He didn't really want to return to that icy cold house. A house without warmth couldn't be a home. Wang Zi-qiang felt unloved and nobody cared about him. For his parents, test scores were the only thing that mattered.

"Hey, you've drifted off. What's on your mind? Where are you going?" A smiling Jian Zhen-guo patted him on the shoulder and asked. Jian and Wang were in the same class. "Xu Wei and I are going shopping at a stationer's shop for some pens and books. Want to come along?" Jian asked Wang.

"I can't. I need to go home to do homework and take simulated tests." Wang said. He really envied Jian Zhen-guo's smiles, relaxation, and freedom.

"It won't take that long. We're also going to eat stinky tofu and noodles. They're lip-smacking." Jian asked again. "Don't you want to go? Let's go!" At that time, the sunny Xu Wei joined them.

真不想回到那個冷冰冰的家，不溫暖的房子怎麼能算是家，沒有人愛的自己就像不存在一樣。沒有人在乎自己，重要的向來只是分數而已。

「想什麼想到恍神啊！等下你要去哪裡？」同班的簡振國經過他身邊，笑著拍了他一下。「我跟徐偉要去逛文具店買筆買書，你要不要一起去？」

「我不能去，要回家寫功課跟測驗卷。」看著簡振國的笑臉，王子強其實很羨慕簡振國的輕鬆自由。

「又不差那一點時間！我們還要一起去吃臭豆腐跟麵線，很好吃哦，你不想去嗎？一起去嘛！」開朗的徐偉也過來湊熱鬧。

"I wish I could, but I really can't." Wang said. "My mom forbids me to eat out. Unless I need to go to cram school after school, I must go home to study or do homework. You guys go ahead." He looked at the two of them walking away bantering and laughing without a care in the world, so he felt his book bag even heavier. He thought that Jian Zhen-guo and Xu Wei would talk behind his back to laugh at him as a bookworm who knew only to study and take tests, but nothing else.

"It sucks to be Wang Zi-qiang, who shoulders a lot of stress but has no friends," Wang Zi-qiang muttered.

He stopped to look at a recyclables collection station irritably, considering the possibility of letting himself loose and totally unrestrained for just a while. He mulled over the consequence of throwing his heavy book bag into the bin like a recyclable.

"Throwing myself into the bin would be even better. Then I wouldn't need to go home to face reality," Wang said to himself. But instead, he put his book bag on the ground entertaining the thought of not being Wang Zi-qiang. "I'd rather be someone else or a speck of dust than Wang Zi-qiang!"

「真的沒辦法，我媽不准我在外面吃東西。放學不補習的話，就要回家讀書寫作業。你們去吧！」看著簡振國跟徐偉兩個人愉快又有說有笑地離開，王子強覺得書包更重了。他認為簡振國跟徐偉一定在背後竊竊私語，嘲笑自己是書呆子，只會死讀書跟考試，其他什麼都不會。

「當王子強真倒楣，壓力大又沒有朋友！」

他停下腳步，煩躁地看著路旁的資源回收分類箱，考慮著任性一下的可能性，評估把沉重的書包狠狠地扔進去後果會如何。

「最好也把我自己丟進去！我就不用回家面對了！」他把書包放在地上，心裡想著真不想再當王子強。「當別人、當灰塵都好，就是不想做王子強！」

"Oh God, someone help me! Make me disappear!" Wang Zi-qiang shouted.

A crisp voice said to him, "Hi, Wang Zi-qiang. My name is Green Fairy, and you can just call me GF."

He was startled and his jaw dropped. "Are they shooting some kind of a practical joke for reality TV?" Wang wondered. He quickly looked around and saw no sign of hidden cameras before turning to look at the pretty lady who had just popped up by the recyclables collection bins out of thin air. Wang unconsciously grabbed his book bag closer.

"Don't you worry. I am in charge of gardens and grounds in heaven, but one day I inadvertently stepped on and crushed seven sprouts. As a punishment, I was sent to this temporal world to accomplish seven missions: to help seven children who emit distress signals for help." Green Fairy said genially. "Wang Zi-qiang, you are my second mission."

You must have mistaken me for somebody else; I never sent out any messages for help," Wang said firmly, shaking his head. His facial expression told Green Fairy that he didn't believe her. But suddenly, Wang blushed because he just remembered that he had indeed shouted out for help right before GF showed up.

「天啊！誰來幫我，讓我消失吧！」王子強仰天長嘆。

「王子強同學，你好！我是綠葉仙子，你可以叫我小綠！」清脆的聲音響起。

是什麼惡作劇的實境秀錄影嗎？嚇了一跳的王子強嘴巴都還沒來得及合攏，趕緊警覺地看看四周，還好沒有發現任何隱藏的攝影機。他回頭瞪著資源回收分類箱旁忽然冒出來的大眼秀氣女生，下意識地把書包拉近自己。

「你不用擔心，我在天界負責園藝工作，因為不小心踩壞了七株幼苗，所以來到人間要完成七個任務，幫助七個發出求救訊號的孩子。」小綠態度很親切。「王子強同學，你是我的第二個任務。」

「你一定是弄錯人了！我可沒發出什麼求救訊號！」王子強堅定地搖頭，表情很抗拒。忽然想到自己剛剛的仰天長嘆，臉上熱熱的忍不住發紅。

"In the tests for this month, you finished third in your school; you scored perfectly in every subject, save math—you missed one question there. Am I right?" GF said, blinking her eyes.

"You're not wrong," Wang replied reluctantly.

"Your mother is very strict with you. She rarely praises you; she just hopes and demands that you achieve more," GF said. "Your father rarely nags you, but he seems to be uninterested in how you feel. Am I right?"

"Do you know my parents?" Wang Zi-qiang asked in surprise.

"As for you, you feel that schooling and learning are just for taking exams; everything you do is to help you score higher. But you're annoyed by that and you hate that," Green Fairy kept talking without answering Wang's question. "At times, you really want to become someone else. You don't want to be Wang Zi-qiang any more; it suits you best if you simply disappear; you don't mind being turned into a speck of dust. Am I right?"

"Hey, these are my secrets. How did you learn all that?" Wang Zi-qiang screamed, almost in horror.

「你這次月考排名全校第三名，幾乎每科都滿分，只有數學錯了一題，對吧！」小綠眨眨眼睛。

「嗯，是沒錯啦！」王子強回答地有點勉強。

「你媽媽管你管得很兇，很少稱讚你，總是希望你好還應該更好；你爸爸很少唸你，但是好像也不太在意你的感受，對吧！」

「你認識我爸媽？」王子強有點驚訝。

「你覺得讀書只為了考試、一切只為了成績、很煩很討厭，有時真希望自己變成別人，不要當王子強了，消失了最好，甚至變成一粒灰塵也好，對吧！」

「那是我的祕密，你怎麼可能知道？」王子強聲音尖銳，臉色十分驚慌。

"I told you that I'm Green Fairy, didn't I?" GF said mischievously. "And fairies know it all."

"My mission is to give you a present and help you," GF said as she reached out her arm and slightly turned her palm. With that, a cloth bag appeared in her palm. She gave the bag to Wang Zi-qiang.

"What's this? I don't take things from a stranger." Arms behind his back, Wang refused to accept the bag.

"Two things are in the bag: an incense stick from heaven and a divine leaf," Green Fairy said. When stars come out, light the incense stick and look at the veins of the leaf attentively. Then allow your mind to follow the veins, and you will see what you hope to see."

"An incense stick from heaven? It can receive signals like radar?" Wang was thinking fast.

"Smart boy," GF said approvingly.

「我説了我是綠葉仙子嘛！」小綠表情有點調皮。「仙子無所不知。」

「我的任務就是要送你一個禮物！並且幫助你。」小綠伸出手掌，翻轉了一下，出現一個布包，要交給王子強。

「這是什麼東西？陌生人的東西不能亂拿！」王子強兩手收在背後，猶豫著不肯收。

「裡面有兩樣東西，一支天香加一片仙葉。」小綠仔細説明。「等星星出來的時候，你點這支天香，然後專心地看著這片葉子上的紋路，讓你的心念跟著葉脈走，你就會看到你希望看到的。」

「天香？像雷達一樣能接受訊息？」王子強思索著。

「聰明的孩子！」小綠的表情很讚賞。

"A divine leaf? People say that veins of leaves are like fingerprints of humans and no two leaves have identical maps of veins," Wang said. Apparently GF's praise got him to power on his brain. He continued. "I've read that in the microcosm of a leaf, you can see a whole world. There's much more to a leaf than meets the eye."

"Are you saying that the leaf you gave me is a 3D virtual image projector that enables me to see what I want to see?" Wang was now very curious.

"Exactly. The divine leaf can take you wherever you want to go. Knowing the past helps you know the future and find the answer you want," GF now looked at Wang Zi-qiang even more approvingly. She handed the cloth bag over to Wang, again.

"All right, I will play with it," Wang said. His curiosity was piqued. He accepted the gift. He couldn't wait to try it out.

"I believe you'll like it," GF said. She smiled at Wang and vanished beside the recyclables collection bins.

「葉子？有人説葉脈就像指紋一樣，沒有兩片葉子的葉脈紋路是完全相同的。」被稱讚的王子強腦袋開始像電腦一樣運轉起來。「書上也有説：一花一世界，一葉一如來。葉子是很有學問的。」

「不過，妳的意思是説，妳送的葉子像立體虛擬投影？可以讓我看到想看到的？」王子強的好奇心被勾起來了。

「沒錯！仙葉可以讓你看到心念所到之處，鑑往知來，找到答案。」小綠以欣賞的眼光看著王子強，再度交出布包。

「好！我實驗看看。」王子強產生興趣，有點躍躍欲試地收下布包。

「相信你會喜歡！」
小綠笑笑，在資源回收分類箱旁失去蹤影。

Wang hurried home and rushed through his homework and simulated tests. He couldn't wait to open the cloth bag, which he had hidden in his book bag. The slender incense stick had an imprinted image of what appeared to be two characters, but it was quite blurred that it was impossible to make out even under a magnifying glass at close range. Under the light, dew drops seemingly rolled every which way on the divine leaf. Wang studied the leaf closely, but still he had no idea what it was.

Wang lit the incense stick. Mentally, he was treating this as a great experiment. He focused on the rising smoke. Indigo-colored light slowly flowed into the leaf. Blue purplish rays of light quickly reached every fine vein of the leaf.

Wang stared at the leaf attentively. The leaf became larger and larger. In the blink of an eye, he was standing in the leaf. The indigo-colored roads, though virtual, appeared quite real. The far side of the picture looked a bit strange as it seemed vast and wide open extending as far as the eye could see. Wang saw many transparent screens floating around with colorful videos and sounds.

回到家，王子強急急忙忙趕著做完功課跟測驗卷，迫不及待地拿出那個藏在書包裡的布包。布包裡那支細長的香，上面好像有兩個字的痕跡，可是就算拿出放大鏡近距離細看，還是看不出究竟寫了什麼字。倒是那片在燈光下好像還有露珠在滾動的綠葉子，研究半天也認不出是什麼植物的葉子。

王子強以在實驗室做實驗的精神專注地點燃了天香，聚精會神看著裊裊向上飄動的煙。燈下的葉子緩緩地注入了靛青色的流光，介於藍色和紫色之間淺淺的藍紫色光線，迅速地流過每一條細細的葉脈與紋路。

王子強睜大眼睛屏息專注地研究著葉子，眼前的葉子越變越大，才一下子，他發現自己竟然站在葉子當中。靛青色的道路虛擬卻很有真實感，看起來好奇怪。遠方看起來好空曠，視野無限延伸出去。眼前浮現一個個透明的薄幕，上面閃動著彩色的聲光與畫面。

First to show up on the screens were Jian Zhen-guo, holding a shopping bag, and Xu Wei. They were chatting.

"Jian Zhen-guo, have you bought all the things that you came to buy?" Xu Wei asked. Seeing Jian's nod, Xu said, "Then I want to buy some snacks and braised dishes."

"Xu Wei, aren't you eating too much? You just finished stinky tofu and two large bowls of vermicelli and you had two orders of vermicelli to go. All this isn't enough?" Jian said.

"But the take-out is for my mom and my sister. Mom is under the weather, so she is resting in bed. I think hot, liquid food will be easier for her to swallow. Also, I am afraid that my sister has yet to have dinner, so I bought her something, too. If she doesn't finish it tonight, the leftover can be served with porridge as our breakfast," Xu Wei explained.

"You're pretty considerate. You take care of your family," Jian said.

首先出現的，是拿著提袋的簡振國跟徐偉正在聊天。

「簡振國，你想買的東西都買到了嗎？」看到對方點頭，徐偉繼續說。「那我還要去買一點小菜跟滷味。」

「徐偉，你也太貪吃了。剛剛才吃完臭豆腐跟大碗的麵線，你還外帶了兩份麵線，這樣還吃不夠啊！」

「沒啦！不是我要吃，是幫我媽跟我妹買的。我媽身體不舒服，躺在床上休息，軟軟熱熱流質的食物比較好吞食。我怕我妹沒吃晚餐，多準備一點。剩下來的明天可以配稀飯當早餐。」

「徐偉，你不錯哦，還會幫忙照顧家人。」

"It's nothing. Dad passed away. Mom is unwell, and my sister is younger than me. I, the big old brother, should do something to take care of them," Xu Wei replied, a little bashful. "Every day, after I've cleaned up, put things away, and done the laundry, I'm already pretty much pooped. Then I have to quickly take a shower and do my homework. I go to bed right after that. Therefore, I have little to no time to study. No wonder my test scores are just barely scraping by," Xu Wei said.

"I really want to give you a hand, but I can hardly keep myself afloat, much less help you," Jian said. "Mom is a new immigrant. It's very hard for her to learn things, so she can't help me. On top of that, I'm not very good at memorizing or comprehending things, so my scores are not much better than yours. Xu Wei, you and I are almost like twins in our circumstances—six of one and half a dozen of the other," Jian shrugged and smiled wryly. Jian, an optimistic sort, didn't forget to find reason for hope. Jian continued, "There's no way you and I can compete with Wang Zi-qiang. He's smart and very hard-working. He aces tests without even breaking a sweat."

"When I am taking a test, I always wish that I were Zang Zi-qiang. Then all test problems would be no problems at all."

「我爸不在了，媽媽生病、妹妹又還小，我是哥哥，出點力幫忙照顧家裡，沒關係啦。」徐偉有點不好意思。「等我忙完家裡的打掃、整理、洗衣服，就很累了。趕緊洗洗澡做完功課就要睡覺了，都沒什麼時間讀書，所以考試成績都勉強在及格邊緣低空飛過！」

「我很想幫你，可惜我自己也是泥菩薩過江，半斤八兩！我媽媽是新住民，她學東西也很辛苦，沒辦法教我。再加上我記憶力不太好、理解力也差，成績比你好不了多少。」簡振國聳聳肩苦笑，樂天的他不忘安慰自己。「我們沒辦法跟王子強比啦，他很聰明也很努力用功，考試要考高分對他來講不難啦。」

「每次考試的時候，我都希望能變成王子強就好了！這樣考卷我就通通會寫了！」

"Whenever the teacher hands out report cards, I wish that Wang Zi-qiang could give me some of his scores." Xu Wei and Jian Zhen-guo chatted as they ordered some braised dishes.

"BTW, Jian Zhen-guo, do you think that Wang Zi-qiang acted a little strange today? I wonder if he is feeling unwell. Let's check on him," Xu Wei said.

"I do. But I just asked him to come along with us. He didn't want to come," Jian Zhen-guo said.
"I'll ask him tomorrow to ride bikes with me on Sunday. It's not good to always stay home studying. It's necessary to go outside and get some sun," Xu Wei said.

Watching his two classmates talking about him on a floating screen, Wang Zi-qiang felt mixed emotions. He didn't know that these two guys would think about him in private. He had wrongly suspected that they would ridicule him behind his back or call him an oddball. It turned out that he had been too distrusting. He didn't realize that the cheerful, optimistic Xu Wei was so capable of doing the chores at home and taking care of his family. Wang had also just learned that Jian Zhen-guo, who always wore a smile, knew that he learned at a slower speed and he envied Wang.

「我是希望發成績單的時候，王子強的分數可以分給我一點！」

徐偉跟簡振國一邊點滷味一邊聊天。

「對了！簡振國，你覺不覺得王子強今天臉色怪怪的，會不會是身體不太舒服？我們關心一下他吧。」

「我也覺得。可是剛剛問他要不要一起來逛逛，吃點東西，他又不想跟來。」簡振國有點無奈。

「我明天再問問他星期天要不要去騎腳踏車好了！老是窩在家裡讀書也不是很好，還是要出來走走曬曬太陽。」

王子強看著薄幕上兩位同學討論著自己，心裡五味雜陳。原來他們默默地在關心自己啊。還以為他們在背後取笑自己是奇怪的異類，原來只是自己多心。還有，他不知道樂觀開朗的徐偉是這麼能幹，還會幫忙做家事照顧家人；總是愛笑的簡振國覺得學習比別人慢，還會羨慕子強。

For the longest time Wang Zi-qiang had thought that it would be easier to be somebody else and that he would have been happier if he had become another person. Not so. Everyone has his own cross to bear.

"There're ways to study better, and I can share with them my ways. I volunteer to be their tutor after school," Wang Zi-qiang said to himself, thinking of Jian Zhen-guo and Xu Wei. "Mom and Dad don't love me anyway. They love only my test scores," Wang continued. "My friends' love is good enough for me."

"Who said that your parents don't love you? You just don't recognize it," said a voice. Then he saw Green Fairy. By now he had grown accustomed to the way GF showed up, so he wasn't at all surprised to see her again.

GF pointed at another thin, transparent screen. Wang Zi-qiang saw his parents on that screen. At the moment, they were in a heated discussion. They seemed to be arguing.

還以為當別人會比較輕鬆幸福，事實是每一個人背後都有自己的辛苦與努力。

「讀書是有方法的，我可以跟他們分享自己的心得，下課後自願當他們的小老師。」王子強自言自語說著。「反正爸爸媽媽不愛我，他們只愛我的考試成績，我有朋友關心就夠了！」

「誰說你爸媽不愛你？只是你不知道而已。」小綠忽然出現在面前，王子強已經很習慣她的出場方式，此刻不再感到驚訝。

小綠指著前方的新薄幕，上面浮現出爸爸跟媽媽的畫面。他們正在熱烈討論，有點像意見不合在爭執。

Wang was a little surprised to see such a scene. His parents had never argued in front of him. They had always been on the same side when they dealt with him: His mother alone would talk, and his father would look on without uttering a word.

"Zi-qiang hasn't looked too well recently, and he has appeared to be unhappier and unhappier," his father, perturbed, said to his mother. "I'm not in favor of the way you've treated Zi-qiang. By scolding, you're putting him under pressure, and I'm afraid that he might do studip things if he's under too much pressure."

"Do you think that I want to scold him? It hurts me when I scold him. He's my son, too," his mother shot back, feeling that she had been wronged. "I don't want to be a stern tiger mom, either, but only under strict discipline can he be nurtured to be a superior student. Everything that I do is for his good."

"You said that there should be no gaps and contradictions between you and me when we guide Zi-qiang. That's why I've gone along with your approach and haven't said things to contradict you," his father said, his worries written all over his face. "But we want him to be well-rounded. Learning should encompass all five ways of life: moral, intellect, physical health, group life, and beauty. You can't focus on test scores alone."

王子強有點意外，平常爸爸媽媽就是一國的，從來沒在自己面前爭吵過。總是媽媽在講話、爸爸保持沉默。

「子強最近氣色不太好，看起來越來越不快樂。我不太贊成你一直用責備罵人的方式管教，這樣他會有壓力。我擔心壓力太大的孩子會想不開。」爸爸皺著眉、神情很苦惱。

「你以為我願意嗎？我的兒子難道我不心疼嗎？」媽媽的表情很委屈。
「我也不想當個疾言厲色的虎媽呀！但是，嚴格的管教才會教出優秀的孩子，一切都是為了他好。」

「因為你說我們兩個人的管教方式不能有落差跟矛盾，這樣的話子強會不知道該怎麼辦，我才配合你、不阻止你。」爸爸的憂慮很明顯。「可是，孩子的成長是全方位的，德智體群美五育都很重要。不能只偏重成績跟分數。」

"I've known since his birth that Zi-qiang is very smart. Gifted children like him must be carefully nurtured and cultivated. It would be a shame if we let him go down a wrong path," his mother said, her helpless eyes looking into the distance. "I became an orphan at a very young age. Later I was adopted, but my adoptive parents could not give me a good education. Consequently, I suffered a lot and missed many opportunities. I will not let that happen to my baby."

"I want Zi-qiang to stand out in a crowd, and I want him to succeed. I want him to have a splendidly wonderful and successful life," his mother continued in a firm voice. "We can't spoil him. Instead, we must put him through hardships and let him learn to be patient. Haven't you heard this adage, 'before heaven will give a person big responsibilities, it first puts him through his paces to evaluate his fitness to take on the responsibilities'? "

"When you think you're protecting him, you're actually harming him," his father replied while shaking his head. "I still think that you have been way too strict with Zi-qiang."

「子強一生下來，我就知道他很聰明優秀。這種資優型的孩子一定要好好栽培，不能讓他走歪走偏了。那就太可惜了！」媽媽看向遠方，眼神很無奈。「我小時候是個孤兒、後來被養父母領養，就是因為環境不好欠栽培，所以我吃了很多苦，也錯失很多機會。我不會讓我的寶貝兒子跟我一樣。」

「我要子強比別人更優秀更出色，我要他出人頭地！我希望他擁有更燦爛更成功的人生！」媽媽的語氣很堅決。「孩子不能寵，要讓他吃苦、學會忍耐！你沒聽過嗎？天將降大任於斯人也，必先苦其心志。」

「愛之適足以害之，我還是覺得你的嚴格要求太過分了！」爸爸搖頭。

His mother also shook her head and said, "I love him a lot, so I ask him to do a lot. It's you who don't know better." She would not be outdone.

Back and forth, the two of them traded punches as the situation got frostier and frostier. Both pushed and defended their view. Neither side would back down an inch.

"Only if a person grew up in plenty of love as a child will he have the empathy to love others and himself as an adult," his father said with a sigh.

His mother was about to refute when she abruptly stopped to think. Then she began to cry.

At this time, the screen started to turn dark and Wang Zi-qiang found that he had returned to his own room from the MR journey. He couldn't begin to describe how shocked he was by what he had just viewed and the contradicting opinions of his mother and father. He never thought that his father's silence might mean anything other than that his father didn't care about him. His father had been silent only so that his parents could have the appearance of a united front on his education and upbringing. He never knew that his mother was an orphan and that had driven her strong desire to help make him successful and stand out in the world.

「愛之深責之切，是你不懂！」媽媽也搖頭。

眼看兩個人的氣氛越來越僵，互相都堅持己見不肯示弱。

「擁有足夠愛的孩子，長大了才有能力愛別人！」爸爸嘆了一口氣，語重心長地繼續說。「也才有能力好好愛自己。」

媽媽張大了嘴巴正準備要好好反駁，忽然間停了下來若有所思，開始淚流不止。

畫面漸漸暗了，王子強發現自己回到了房間，他無法形容內心的震驚。原來爸爸媽媽是這樣想的。他沒有想過爸爸的沉默不是不在乎，而是為了配合媽媽的管教；也不知道媽媽小時候是個孤兒，所以特別希望孩子能出人頭地。

"Do you know why your mother cried?" Green Fairy asked Wang Zi-qiang. She believed that, as smart as he was, he would know.

"I kind of know," Wang Zi-qiang lowered his head and his eyes were moist and red. "I think my mother didn't have a very happy childhood. I should comfort her. I will also tell my father that he does not need to worry about me and that I'm fine. I will take good care of myself."

"I just know that you'll get it," GF said with relief.

"Look. The incense stick has about finished burning. Take a look at the words that it has given to you and you alone," GF said, her eyes were a little ted too. "I should go now. I've accomplished my second mission."

"Thank you, GF," Wang Zi-qiang said. He was a little anxious, and he really wanted to talk to GF a lot more. "Will you take the leaf back? Or perhaps it will disappear momentarily?"

「你懂得你媽媽為什麼掉眼淚嗎？」小綠心裡覺得：以王子強的聰慧應該會明白。

「我好像知道……」王子強低著頭，眼眶也紅了。「我想，我媽的童年應該不是很快樂。我應該好好安慰她。也要告訴爸爸，不用擔心，我很好。我也會把我自己照顧好。」

「我就知道你會懂。」小綠的神情很欣慰。

「對了！天香快燒完了，看看天香留給你的字吧，那是專屬於你的訊息。」小綠眼眶也有點紅。「我該離開了，我的第二個任務也完成了。」

「小綠謝謝你。」王子強有點焦急，其實他內心想多跟小綠講一會兒話。「葉子你會帶走嗎？還是等一下也會消失？」

"The divine leaf came from heaven, so of course it will not stay in the temporal world for long. It will wither in a moment," GF said. Her own image gradually turned transparent. "Some things disappear with time, but other things never will," GF said her final message.

The incense stick had completely burned up. Two characters vaguely appeared in the ashes: Growing up. The indigo light in the veins was now all gone.

Green Fairy was nowhere to be seen, but her voice echoed, "Wang Zi-qiang, you're a smart boy, so grow up bravely. Know to love others and yourself. You'll have a happy life. Bless you!"

「葉子來自天界，當然不會長留人間。接下來就會開始枯萎。」小綠的影子慢慢變透明。「有些東西會隨時間消失，有些東西永遠不會。」

天香燃燒殆盡。灰燼裡若隱若現出現兩個字：成長。葉脈上靛青色的流光已全部消失。

小綠的影像不見了，但她的聲音像回音般迴盪：「王子強，你是個聰明的好孩子，勇敢地長大吧！懂得愛人與愛自己，你的人生一定會很幸福的！祝福你！」

第三個任務
Mission Three

好想當網紅
A social media influencer dream

"It's wonderful to be a social media influencer. People admire her every move!"

"It must feel great to the center of attention."

After thinking thoughts like these, Fang Ya-ping took a mirror during recess to a spot behind a bush on campus where her chances of being seen by her schoolmates was the lowest because it's the least visited place within the confines of the school. She held the mirror up with her right hand as if raising a torch of hope.

Fang Ya-ping walked around smiling while looking in the mirror, trying to find the angle where she looked best. She waved her left and began to talk about some imaginary trees.

"Hi, there. I am Fang Ya-ping. I wanted to share with you today an urban legend going around on campuses."

「當網紅真好，一舉一動都是別人的目光焦點！」

「很多人關注的感覺一定很棒！」

下課時間，方雅蘋拿著鏡子匆匆跑到校園樹叢後面，找個同學最少去的角落開始練習。右手高舉鏡子，好像舉著希望的火炬般。

方雅蘋一面走動一面看著鏡中的自己微笑著，試著找到自己最迷人的角度。她努力笑著揮舞左手，介紹身旁想像中的樹。

「我是方雅蘋，今天我想要分享一個校園裡的都市傳説。」

"This is a Taiwan crepe myrtle. Isn't it gorgeous? It's also called crepe myrtle of the south. It's a deciduous tree. It's easiest to recognize it by its trunk. It's got brown barks with white spots. The barks are so smooth that they seem to be in a thin layer of waxy coating, making it quite slippery. In fact, it's so slippery that monkeys, the tree-climbing experts, can't climb the tree without losing their grips and falling down the tree. Therefore, the tree is also called monkey-slepping...er...monkey-slipping tree or monkey...monkey-shying tree. There's a story about Taiwan crepe myrtle...."

Fang Ya-ping stopped her in-front-of-a-mirror monologue to clear her throat and repeated monkey-slipping tree and monkey-shying tree several times—two terms that had made her tongue-tied moments before. She was quite upset about her own performance and her inability to say just a few sentences fluently. She felt her monologue had been like a little kid reciting a passage: stiff and not at all vivid.

"Every move of a charming social media influencer must captivate the audience everywhere. How difficult can it be?" Fang Ya-ping felt terrible that she had been unable to nail the practice in front of a mirror. She knew that she had a very long way to go before she could advance to recording on her cell phone or broadcasting live.

「你們看到我旁邊的這棵九芎，很漂亮吧！它還有另一個美麗的名字南紫薇。」

「九芎是落葉喬木，它的樹幹是最容易辨認的部分，樹皮是褐色夾雜著白色的塊斑，非常光亮平滑，好像上過一層蠟一樣，就連擅長爬樹的猴子都會被滑下來呢，所以又叫做猴滑樹、猴不爬。關於這棵樹有一個故事……」

方雅蘋清了清嗓、重複著「猴滑樹」、「猴不爬」這兩個讓自己舌頭打結的詞句，一邊懊惱著。就這麼幾句台詞，可是偏偏就是講不順；很像小學生背書一樣，超生硬的、一點都不生動。

「想當個充滿魅力、舉手投足都能抓住大家眼球的網紅，有這麼難嗎？」

方雅蘋覺得自己很遜。連用鏡子練習都結結巴巴講成這樣，想要進階到用手機錄影或開直播，還有好長一大段路要走。

That this wasn't her first practice made her feel even more terrible. She had practiced in a low volume in front of the mirror in school restrooms. Her schoolmates mocked her for that:

"This isn't your home, and the mirror is not for your exclusive use. Why are you occupying it for so long? " went one schoolmate.

"Fang Ya-ping, don't you feel yourself too much?" another schoolmate said. "Or perhaps you take that as a magic mirror that will say you're the fairest of all in the world? Could that be you?"

"You want to be a social media influencer? Haven't you seriously checked your own looks and eloquence? Yes, you do need to look into the mirror, but you should go home and do that to your heart's content," sneered yet another schoolmate.

Fang Ya-ping recalled such contemptuous words, every one of which penetrated like an arrow. Ouch, that hurt.

想起之前她在女生廁所的鏡子前小聲練習，還被其他女同學冷冷嘲笑。

「鏡子不是妳家的，也不是妳專用的，妳幹嘛霸占這麼久！」

「方雅蘋，妳也太自戀了吧！還是妳當這面鏡子是魔鏡，會告訴妳世界上誰最美麗？會是妳嗎？哈！」

「想當網紅也不考慮自己的顏值跟口才？鏡子是該照，但妳應該是回家自己好好照個夠啦！」

像這樣的冷言冷語，好比一支一支箭射了過來，好痛！

Fang Ya-ping, infuriated, couldn't help shaking. She gritted her teeth and vowed to find a shortcut to internet fame with which she could show all those people who had doubted her and her dream how wrong they had been. Their jaws would drop and they would be sorry.

She looked upward toward heaven and shouted, "I want to be a social media influencer!"

Suddenly, all the hustle and bustle around her stopped. Even the trees and leaves that had been waving in the breeze became motionless.

"Howdy, Fang Ya-ping. I am Green Fairy. Just call me GF," A crispy voice came through from behind the trees.

Fang Ya-ping was startled and couldn't say a word to continue her practice of the urban legend spreading on campus, which was nonsense that she herself had fabricated based on not a thread of reality. The way this lady who just talked to Fang showed up was really like magic. Where on earth did she come from? Fang Ya-ping rubbed her eyes and shook her head in confusion.

方雅蘋忍不住氣得發抖，她咬牙決心要找到大紅大紫的捷徑，讓那些看不起她的人全都跌破眼鏡！

她仰天大喊著：「我想當網紅！」

忽然間四周喧鬧的聲音都靜止了。連風中搖曳的樹枝與樹葉也不再晃動。

「方雅蘋同學，妳好！我是綠葉仙子，妳可以叫我小綠！」清脆的聲音從樹叢裡響起。

方雅蘋愣住了，一句話也說不出來。剛剛差點要練習繼續講下去的校園都市傳說，完全是自己準備亂掰的故事；真的是隨口說說，一點根據都沒有的。可是，這位找自己講話的秀氣女生，出場的方式還真像是什麼魔幻故事。她到底是從哪裡冒出來的？方雅蘋忍不住揉揉眼睛，疑惑地搖晃著腦袋。

"Don't you worry. I am in charge of gardens and grounds in heaven, but one day I inadvertently stepped on and crushed seven sprouts. As a punishment, I was sent to this temporal world to accomplish seven missions: to help seven children with whom I have a predestined connection," Green Fairy said in a sweet voice. "Fang Ya-ping, you're my third mission."

"This GF lady is better suited to be a social media influencer than me," Fang Ya-ping thought to herself. "Nice skin, pretty face, unique clothes, genteel, and eloquent, and her story is extraordinarily bizarre."

"Are you broadcasting live? Am I on?" Fang Ya-ping asked excitedly while sizing up GF, trying to find where she had hidden her camera, and wondering what GF would ask her to do on her program.

Fang Ya-ping's heart raced and breath quickened, waiting for GF to talk.

「妳不用擔心，我在天界負責園藝工作，因為不小心踩壞了七株幼苗，所以來到人間要幫助七個有緣的孩子。」小綠聲音很好聽。「方雅蘋同學，妳是我的第三個任務。」

跟自己比起來，這位小綠更有資格當網紅。外型很有氣質，皮膚好、五官也精緻漂亮，服裝很特別，口才也不錯，最重要的是——她的故事超離奇。

「妳在直播什麼節目嗎？我上了節目嗎？」方雅蘋有點興奮地研究小綠，隱藏式鏡頭到底藏在什麼地方？節目內容是小綠到校園玩整人遊戲嗎？還是小綠準備要逼自己完成什麼指令？

方雅蘋心跳得好快，呼吸也加速，等著小綠開口。

"You want to be a social media influencer, don't you?" Green Fairy asked Fang, shocking Fang right away.

"Do you understand what a social media influencer is?"

"Have you figured out what a social media influencer thinks deep down?"

"Are you crystal clear on the real reason why you want to be a social media influencer?"

Instead of explaining the rules for playing on her live broadcast, Green Fairy lobbed one question after another at Fang Ya-ping in rapid succession.

To be completely honest, Fang Ya-ping had yet to settle down to think through those questions. All along she had simply admired the influence that a social media influencer could wield. She had never thought anything beyond that simple admiration.

Green Fairy handed an elongated cloth bag to Fang Ya-ping, who was now deep in thought.

"It's my mission to give you a present and help you think through these questions," Green Fairy said. "Two things are in this bag: an incense stick and a divine leaf."

「妳想當網紅對不對？」小綠一問，方雅蘋當場傻住了。

「妳了解網紅嗎？」

「妳知道網紅的內心世界在想什麼嗎？」

「妳知道自己想當網紅的真正原因嗎？」

沒想到小綠說出來的不是解釋節目或遊戲說明，而是丟出一個又一個問題。

說真的，這些問題方雅蘋都沒有靜下心來好好想過。她只是很單純地羨慕網紅的影響力，沒想那麼多。

看著陷入沉思的雅蘋，小綠遞出一個長型布包。

「我的任務就是要送妳一個禮物！幫助妳看清楚想明白。」小綠流暢地介紹著。「這裡面有兩樣東西，一支天香跟一片仙葉。」

"Wait till deep into the night to light this incense stick. Then look at this leaf attentively, allowing your mind to follow the light in its veins, and you will see what you want to know."

Just then a ring sounded. The recess had ended. Trees and leaves began to move in the breeze again. Fang Ya-ping took the cloth bag and went back to her classroom on the double.

As she ran toward her classroom, she thought excitedly, "Could this possibly be the gift that I have dreamed about day and night— 'The Secrets of Becoming A Social Media Influencer Instantly'?'"

After returning home that evening, Fang Ya-ping had thought about postponing till later to start doing her homework so that she could just open the cloth bag at once to study what was inside, but she thought better of it after recalling what Green Fairy had told her. Therefore she did her homework and waited till deep into the night to open the bag.

The incense stick didn't seem to be anything remarkable except perhaps something was written on the stick. But that something was so blurry that, for the life of her, Fang Ya-ping couldn't make out if it was characters or numbers. The divine leaf, vibrant under the light, bore a resemblance to the facial mask that one influencer had recommended for facial care. Both were shiny and striking.

「深夜裡妳再點這支天香，然後專心地看著這片葉子，讓妳的心跟著葉脈上出現的光線遊走，妳就會看到妳想知道的。」

上課鈴聲響起，樹枝與樹葉又開始恢復了晃動，方雅蘋接下了布包，急急忙忙衝回教室。

她一邊奔跑一邊興奮地想：「難道……難道……這個禮物就是我每天早晚都夢想要得到的──網紅速成祕笈？」

回到家，方雅蘋本來打算晚點再寫功課，想直接先拆開布包，偷偷研究一下。後來她想到小綠的提醒，還是乖乖寫完作業，等到深夜才迫不及待地拿出布包。

布包裡那支細長的香，看起來好像很普通，上面有模糊的字跡，看了半天也看不出到底是文字還是數字。燈光下鮮活的綠葉子，倒是像敷過哪個網紅推薦的面膜一樣，閃閃動人。

Fang Ya-ping lit the incense stick with reverence. Almost forgetting to breathe, she stared at the smoke hovering up. The leaf under the light began to show purple light slowly flowing into a web of intricate veins.

Fang Ya-ping saw the leaf getting bigger and bigger like a soft, warm, and comfortable purple carpet quickly extending infinitely in all directions. Fang Ya-ping saw bare feet stepping on the purple carpet and a spotlight shining brightly ahead. Though in a strange place, Fang was not at all afraid and she moved forward.

In front of her, many transparent screens began to float around with colorful videos and sounds. The first to show on the screens was Little Duck, one of her favorite social media influencers.

Little Duck had often broadcast live from many places featuring local dishes or presenting herself in the most fashionable clothes of the time. The featured dishes always seemed to give off delicately sweet aromas that made the audience feel that they ad to try those dishes soon; otherwise, they would fall behind the times and be left with an inexplicable sense of loss.

方雅蘋以虔敬的心情點燃了天香，屏氣凝神地緊盯著盤旋而上的煙。燈下的葉子柔紫色流光緩緩地遊走，紫光灌入填滿每一絲葉脈交錯的紋路裡。

方雅蘋眼前的葉子越來越大，像幅觸感柔軟又溫暖舒適的紫色地毯一樣，迅速地向四面八方無限延伸。方雅蘋低頭看著自己的光腳踩在紫色地毯上面，有一盞閃亮的聚光燈在前方照耀。雖然四周都很陌生，但是她一點也不驚慌，一步步向前方走去。

眼前慢慢浮現透明的薄幕，上面閃動著彩色的聲光與畫面。首先出現的，是自己很喜歡的網紅「小鴨」。

小鴨經常到各地出外景，開直播介紹當地美食，也示範各種時尚流行的穿著打扮。她介紹的食物總是讓人覺得好香好美味，似乎沒吃到就會落伍，還會有種莫名遺憾的感覺。

Her hair was often dyed different colors such as gray-blue, pink, golden, or mixed color. Stylish tattoos decorated her body. She sometimes wore bright headscarves or scarves and donned hot shorts, holey pants, baggy pants, or clothes that exposed her belly button. Her bold and daring clothes would set fashion trends and spur discussions, driving her fans, females and males alike, crazy to copy her.

"Thank you for watching. For friends who support Little Duck, please be sure to Like and turn on the little bell. Also remember to subscribe to my channel. You are also welcome to the fan group of my Facebook to like. See you next time!" Little Duck's signature confident smile and bright eyes reappeared on the screen. No doubt about it. That was Little Duck. No doubt about that.

Fang Ya-ping looked at the familiar face on the thin screen feeling very happy. She wanted to be a social media influencer so much precisely because she was obsessed with Little Duck. She admired Little Duck's self-confidence, kindness, and good looks. She deeply trusted Little Duck's every word as she would an old friend.

不論是染成灰藍色、粉紅色、金黃色、彩色，常常變色的頭髮；還是身上時髦的刺青紋身；或是鮮豔亮麗的頭巾領巾、熱短褲、洞洞褲、垮褲、露出肚臍的中空裝；她那些大膽前衛的造型打扮風格，都會帶動一陣子風潮與話題，讓粉絲團的迷哥迷妹興起一股旋風式的跟風。

「謝謝大家的觀賞，支持小鴨的朋友別忘了按讚跟開啟小鈴鐺，也要記得訂閱我的頻道；也歡迎到小鴨臉書的粉絲團按讚，我們下次見！」招牌的自信笑容與閃亮眼神再度出現，真的是小鴨沒錯！

方雅蘋看著薄幕上熟悉的臉孔，心裡非常開心。她之所以這麼想當網紅，就是因為迷上了小鴨。她很欣賞小鴨的自信、親切、帥氣。就像信任一個熟識的好朋友，方雅蘋深信小鴨所說的話。

New images emerged on the thin screen.

"Are we off the air? Good. The live broadcast is over, and I can stop acting," shouted Little Duck. The thin screen swayed and wrinkled by the breeze, making Little Duck look a little different. Her face became gloomy as if dark clouds had blocked out the sun.

"Give me a break! You packed in so many dishes. You wanted to make me puke? Those were lousy dishes, but I had to pretend and say they were rare delicacies so good that I couldn't stop eating them. This is very hard work for me; it's torture for me," Little Duck said to the person next to her who looked like her boyfriend and assistant, but she sounded very rude.

"I've worked so hard, so you remember to charge those stores a little more for leading customers to them, or twist their arms to get some freebies, coupons, or takeout food. If they don't comply, I am going to give them negative reviews," Little Duck continued in a mean voice. She was arrogant and impatient.

「好了沒！直播已經結束了，我也不用演了！」被風吹皺的薄幕飄動著，讓小鴨的臉看起來有點不太一樣；好像太陽忽然被烏雲遮蔽了，失去了陽光的臉顯得有點陰沉。

「真是的，安排這麼多食物，你是要我吃到吐嗎？」
「明明不好吃，卻要我假裝是難得的美味，還要一口接一口停不下來，我演得很辛苦！難過死了！」
小鴨對著旁邊看起來像是男朋友兼助理的人說話，語氣很不客氣！

「我這麼辛苦，你記得跟店家多收一點業配費用，或者多拗一點禮物、優待券或外帶。那些不答應的小氣店家，再好吃都直接給負評！」
小鴨的聲音很刻薄，態度也很狂傲不耐煩。

"These things are annoying me to death. I dyed my hair only to remove the dye a little later, and then I repeated the process for different colors. I've had perms very frequently. So much so that recently I've lost my hair like crazy. I've had to hide my balding spots from the camera. I'll change my hairdo next time. Perhaps put on a hat or tie a headscarf," Little Duck continued.

"What about clicks and subscriptions? The numbers aren't going up? Teetering on a plateau? You need to come up with some ideas for the live broadcasts! I alone can't take all the load and stress. Give me some fresh, first-rate themes. Status quo isn't going to cut it. I want to be different from the rest of the crowded pack! I want to attract attention and lead the discussion," Little Duck unloaded on her boyfriend.

She continued, "Find some spots where photographing is prohibited or access is controlled, and we will go there for our shows. The more dangerous and restrictive a location is, the more we can excite our followers."

"Anyway, our fans are a whole bunch of morons, oddballs, or eccentrics. The more sensational and outlandish our shows are, the more they love us. So, give me some ideas," Little Duck preached and demanded.

「煩死了！頭髮染了很快又洗掉、洗掉了很快又再染。燙髮頻率也很高，害我最近一直狂掉頭髮！鏡頭前要遮一下避一下，下次該改改造型，換成戴帽子，或綁頭巾好了！」

「最近點閱人數跟訂閱數怎樣？一直沒有增加嗎？差不多到了瓶頸？煩死了，你都不出點主意，要把壓力都讓我承受嗎？想點新鮮的主題吧！不要都是老招，我要跟別人都不一樣！要能引起討論或話題的！」

「你再打聽一下哪邊是禁止攝影或管制的，我們去闖闖。越危險的地方越少人挑戰，這樣才刺激嘛！」

「反正那些粉絲都很宅，越聳動越作怪的題材他們越愛，你也來出點主意吧！」

Fang Ya-ping couldn't believe what she had just witnessed. Little Duck's exaggerated facial expressions still lingering on the screen, Fang Ya-ping felt weakness in her legs, and she almost collapsed onto the soft, purple carpet. Little Duck had been Fang Ya-ping's beloved heroine and idol who explored new frontiers, but now Little Duck had just revealed her true nature: nothing more than a snobbish, vulgar woman who would do anything to get likes and subscriptions and take advantage of others. Life is nothing if not full of twists and turns, but still Fang Ya-ping found the discovery hard to swallow.

Someone once said, "When illusions end, growth begins."
But no one ever told Fang that disillusion could be so bitter and painful.

"No, that's not my Little Duck. No way!" Fang Ya-ping shook her head violently, feeling like crying as she fell into denial.

Just then Fang heard a voice. "Not all social media influencers are like that. Little Duck is just one of the bad apples. Most influencers work exceedingly hard to nurture their domains." Green Fairy said as she walked slowly under the spotlights toward Fang Ya-ping. As the spotlights sent purple light onto the screens, new images began to appear.

方雅蘋看著薄幕上小鴨誇張的表情特寫，兩腳都軟了，差點跌坐在地上，還好地上是軟軟的紫色地毯。那個心目中像似有著開疆闢土氣勢的女英雄、也是偶像的小鴨，此時此刻卻成了不擇手段只想紅、愛占人便宜的俗氣勢利鬼。怎麼會這樣呢？

曾經有人說過：幻滅是成長的開始。
但是沒人提過：幻滅的滋味，竟然是這麼苦澀。

「這不是小鴨！這不是我心目中的那個小鴨！」方雅蘋猛搖著頭，有種想哭的感覺。

「不是所有網紅都是這樣的！這是極少數的例子。很多人是非常努力地在耕耘與經營這塊園地。」聚光燈下，小綠緩緩迎面走來，四周透明的薄幕被聚光燈投射紫光後，開始出現一個又一個畫面。

"In this episode, we want to talk about the sci-fi movie that was just released," said an online movie critic, another social media influencer. "Let's divide this up. Let's take careful notes during and after the movie. We then sort out key points and discuss them together. The key points of the notes should be clear and detailed, and the features and advantages should be captured."

After they had watched the movie, they got together. The team got into heated discussions. The movie critic had taken notes that filled the pages.

"You are the editor of our critique footage. Be sure to captivate the audience's visual attention and to the point," suggested the movie critic. "Let's give it a fast rhythm, and don't make it too lofty so we can address a wide range of audiences. The audio in this section could use a little boost to be more emotionally connected with our audience."

The director and editor of the short film discussed the short film and modified it as they went while the movie critic—the influencer—was racking his brains to write the voice over and tweeted what he was going to say in his critique.

「這一集設定的主題是談剛剛上映的科幻電影，我們分工一下，去看完電影做筆記後再把重點整理整理，一起討論。筆記重點要清楚詳細，把特色跟優點都抓出來。」

影片介紹的小組正在熱烈討論。影評型網紅的筆記密密麻麻都是重點。

「你是剪接師，希望你就視覺部分抓住觀眾眼球，又要能切中主題。節奏也要明快，不要讓我們的評論曲高和寡。這段的音效可以再加強，會更能勾動觀眾情緒。」

短片的編導跟剪接師針對短片進行討論修改。短評影片型網紅正在絞盡腦汁寫旁白台詞，調整寫稿的內容。

The influencer said to his staff, "Please rest assured that we're a team and I'm not much of a fan of individualism. If you feel that our critique film is not good enough, I welcome your input in our brain-storming session."

The thin transparent screens floating in midair now switched to another, unrelated team of people.
A group of actors and actresses were rehearsing a comedy skit. They went over it again and again to get the kinks out and make their performance better.

"When we encounter ridicules or vicious criticisms from sharp-tongued netizens, let's not take them on their face value as that will chip away our confidence and unravel our team spirit. Don't let every little comment from just any Joe Blow rattle it. It's hardly professional if you replace the main actor or actress in the play simply because some people say they're ugly or rustic. Our first consideration should be their ability to act," said a team member during a meeting of the group.

The group was talking about how they should respond to online comments. Team members were focused and enthusiastic as they listened or spoke.

「你放心，我們是團體，我不會堅持個人主義，如果覺得短片劇本不夠好，歡迎加入現場，互相激盪出火花來加分。」

趣味短劇的小組正在彩排。演員一而再、再而三的練習，研究修改表演的方式。

「對網路酸民的嘲諷與惡意評論，不要通通照單全收，會打擊信心、影響我們的士氣。不要人家隨便說，我們馬上站不穩，就隨便相信。人家說女主角醜我們就換女主角，說男主角土我們就改男主角，這是不專業的。演技才是優先考量的。」

舞台劇的小組針對網路留言討論因應方式。工作人員專注而熱情地傾聽與發表意見。

"We must believe in our professionalism and hold firm on our purpose and commitment. If we're doing the right thing, we stay the course. If there's a misunderstanding, step forward and explain clearly. If there're good suggestions, we should adopt them the best we can. Constructive criticism helps fuel us forward," said another member.

The thin transparent screens floating in midair now switched to yet another, unrelated team of people.
The animation team was quite happy with their product as team members watched and discussed their film—the fruit of their labor—in the audio recording room.

"Though some may believe that exaggerated and pointed topics attract attention, I still insist on positive, sunny, and warm topics and approaches. I hope that my film will deliver to its audience positive energy and a shot in the arm to face the predicaments of life."

This type of knowledge-based influencers value the quality of their influence more than the quantity of their business income.

「我們要相信自己的專業與堅持，對的方向就要維持。如果是誤會就出面好好解釋，如果有好的建議就盡量採納。良性的刺激是進步的動能！」

動畫說故事的小組對於成品很滿意，大夥在錄音室裡邊看影片邊討論。

「雖然人家說誇張尖銳的題材才能引起注意，但我還是堅持正面陽光的話題與溫暖的路線。我希望我的影片能讓觀看的人接收到正能量。得到面對人生困境的勇氣。」

知識型網紅堅持質的影響勝過量的豐收。

"I mean every word I say in front of the camera. I recommend a dish only if it is really good. I hope that my audience will feel how I feel. When I talk into the camera, I'm talking to my friends. They know me, but I may not know them yet. Still, I cherish their friendship."

Some social media influencers are careful about what they say because they know their words wield much power.

"Social media influencers are not a profession for money or fame. Rather, it is an undertaking that calls for serious dedication. Every topic I cover entails much work for me to collect comments and viewpoints from all angles. I don't want to mislead my audience."

Some other social media influencers diligently research their topics and otherwise prepare for their shows ahead of time.

After watching all this, Fang Ya-ping remained silent for quite a long while.

Green Fairy asked her gently, "Have you sorted it out? Do you know why you want to be a social media influencer?"

「我面對鏡頭説的每一句話都是我的真心話。真的好吃我才推薦。我希望觀眾能夠感受我內心真正的感受。我面對的不是鏡頭，而是朋友。你認識我，我還不認識你，但我珍惜你當我朋友。」

有的網紅很愛惜羽毛，認為説出口的每一句話都具有重量。

「網紅不是賺錢賺名的職業，而是一份認真投入的事業。針對這個主題，我要蒐集各種角度的評論與看法，以免讓觀眾被誤導而產生偏差。」

也有網紅認真老實做功課與事前準備。

方雅蘋靜靜地沉默了好一陣子。

小綠緩緩地問：「想清楚了嗎？妳為什麼想當網紅？」

After pausing a few moments thinking about it, Fang Ya-ping slowly answered, "If one becomes a social media influencer, it means that even young people can be very good, too. And that person's hard work and success can be appreciated by lots of people in a heartbeat."

Fang Ya-ping continued, "A social media influencer can exert influence over many people, and she can transmit confidence to the timid, people who don't have friends, and those who lack confidence in themselves by making them feel if Fang Yu-ping can succeed in this, so can they."

Fang Ya-ping sighed as she gently said, "I thought that by working hard to learn from my idols would make me as outstanding and charming as my idols."

Green Fairy smiled mysteriously, "Why just learn from your idols? Why not surpass them? Or become a social media influencer yourself?"

方雅蘋思考了一會兒，慢慢回答。

「如果能當上網紅，代表年輕人也可以很優秀，而我的努力與成功，也能一下子就被大家看到。」

「還有，當上網紅，可以影響更多的人；讓膽小的、沒朋友的、沒自信的人，都覺得連我都能成功了、那他們肯定也可以。」

方雅蘋嘆了一口氣，輕輕地説。

「我以為努力跟我的偶像學習，我也能像偶像一樣出色有魅力。」

小綠神祕燦爛地笑：「為什麼妳只能學偶像、像偶像？而不是超越偶像？或成為偶像？」

"Guess who this is," GF continued.

On a thin transparent screen, a mature and confident lady stood at the chairperson's podium in the distance. A wireless microphone sent her fluent speech, given bilingually in Chinese and English, to the loudspeakers. She is too far away, so Fang Ya-ping couldn't tell who she was. Many in the capacity crowd in the conference looked at the speaker with admiration and some nodded their agreement.

Fang Ya-ping trembled ever so slightly as if a miniscule electric current had just passed through her. She was startled and she found that she was in her own room. What she had seen moments before now seemed so real. It's like a dream.

"The incense stick will soon burn up. You can look at the message that it left just for you," GF said. "It's time that moved on. I've accomplished my third mission."

Fang Ya-ping didn't feel like letting Green Fairy go. "Thank you, GF," she said.

「猜猜看，那位到底是誰呢？」

薄幕上，遙遠的主席台上一位成熟有自信的女生，透過無線麥克風以流利中英文傳達著重要訊息。距離太遠了，看不清她的臉，只看到研討會現場萬頭騷動景象，觀眾席間許多人的眼神帶著點佩服與仰慕，也有人點頭表示認同。

方雅蘋忽然心頭一動，身上像是有一股非常非常微弱的電流流竄。嚇了一跳的她，忽然發現自己仍在房間。剛剛發生的一切，如真似幻，好像夢境一般。

「天香馬上要燒完了，妳可以看看天香留給妳的專屬特別訊息。」小綠笑了一笑。「是該離開的時候了，我的第三個任務也完成囉。」

方雅蘋有點依依不捨。

「小綠，謝謝妳。」

"The divine leaf will soon wither," GF said as she gradually faded out of sight. "Don't be perturbed by disillusion, but rather be happy by your growth."

The incense stick was now completely burned up. Through its light gray ashes showed two characters: Steady orientation.

The soft purple light in the veins of the divine leaf had now totally disappeared.

Though Green Fairy was nowhere to be seen, her voice echoed, "Fang Ya-ping, when you see a person wiser than you, try to be like that person. When you see a person lesser in character, remind yourself never to fall prey to that person's character defects. You will find your direction and become a model for other people. I cheer for you."

「對了！提醒妳：葉子一會兒就會開始枯萎。」小綠的影子慢慢消失。「不要為幻滅苦惱，要學會因成長而喜悅哦。」

天香燃燒完了，淺淺的灰燼裡隱隱出現兩個字：定位。

葉脈上柔紫色的流光已全部消失。

小綠的影像不見了，但她的聲音仍繚繞著：「方雅蘋，見賢思齊、見不賢內自省。妳會找到自己的方向，成為別人的榜樣的。加油！」

第四個任務
Mission Four

說不出口的需求
The unspeakable

"Can fighting solve your problems?"

"You again! Why can't you talk instead of fight?"

"Fighting, fighting every day. What's wrong with you?"

"If you insist on not talking, I'll put you in a timeout in the hall. You will stand there to think it over. You can come back into the classroom after you have decided to have your father come in and the two of you will apologize."

Xie You-qing was furious all the way home. He slammed his book bag on an end table in the living room.

"What a rotten day!"

"It just came out of blue, damn it!" Xie You-qing was still fuming. "No one could argue that's my fault. It was Li Yu-wei. He started it all."

Xie You-qing had paid for a video game console that had just come out with the gift certificate that his father had given him for his birthday. He adored this latest console. During a recess, Li Yu-wei wanted to borrow it, but Xie You-qing refused. That cheeky Li Yu-wei reached out his hand for it anyway.

「動手打架可以解決事情嗎？」

「又是你！為什麼你就不能好好用說的？非要動手嗎？」

「整天打架鬧事！你到底有什麼問題？」

「你再倔強不說，就到教室外面罰站！」

「站到你想清楚、決定要帶你爸一起來道歉了，再進來上課！」

謝佑青一臉火氣回到家，用力把書包摔在客廳的茶几上。

「今天真是個超級倒楣的壞日子！」

「莫名其妙！可惡！」謝佑青忿忿不平。「明明就不是我的錯！是那個李昱維先找碴的！」

爸爸給的生日禮券，自己拿去換最新一代的電玩遊戲機，寶貝得不得了！就在下課時，李昱維說他要借看。不肯給他，還厚臉皮伸手過來要拿。

"He didn't pay for it, so he had no right to use it," Xie You-qing said. When Xie wasn't watching, Li snatched it from Xie and later Xie dropped it on the ground.

"That served him right. He thought I was timid and could be bossed around," said Xie You-qing as he continued to vent. "See if he dares to provoke me ever again."

"It's only a matter of an eye for an eye. Some people were just asking for a good thrashing," snorted Xie You-qing. "An actor in a Japanese TV drama once said he would return the favor ten fold, even a hundred fold. I only gave him back double the insult that he had thrown at me, so I was quite restrained."

Standing outside the classroom in timeout was indeed a little humiliating, but after a few times, Xie You-qing had gotten quite used to that. During recess, everyone was horsing around except Xie You-qing who just stood there. Some curious Georges even approached him and asked him this and that.

"Xie You-qing, what did you do again that got you this punishment?" asked one.
"Skip class? Didn't do your homework? Being a nuisance? Vandalism? Stealing? Fight?" they asked Xie.

「又不是他花錢買的東西，憑什麼碰？」沒想到這個小子，竟然趁自己不注意時搶走遊戲機，還摔在地上！

「活該！以為我膽小好惹嗎？不知道我很勇敢嗎？以後還敢再招惹我嘛！」

「我只不過是以牙還牙、以眼還眼、加倍奉還而已！有些人就是欠揍。」謝佑青從鼻孔冷冷哼了一聲。「人家日本電視劇的明星說十倍奉還百倍奉還，我算客氣了，才加倍！」

站在教室外面罰站，是有點丟臉，但次數一多，也習慣了。下課時間，大家都在跑跳追逐，只有自己乖乖站著。還有人搞不清楚情況，跑過來東問西問。

「謝佑青，你又幹了什麼事被老師罰站？」
「蹺課？不寫功課？搗蛋？破壞公物？偷東西？打架？」

Xie just ignored them.

However, ignoring his father would not be an option at home. "How am I going to break this news to Dad?" Xie thought to himself. "Perhaps ask him to make time to go to school with me to apologize to the teacher and Li Yu-wei's parents?" But Xie couldn't imagine that even his father could take it lying down.

The thought of being scolded or even beaten by his father made Xie You-qing feel scared...or excited. Xie You-qing's father was very busy, often in a hurry. The two of them had infrequently seen each other, much less had time for some heart-to-heart. It was a treat for Xie You-qing if his father looked at him for a few more moments or listened to him talk about things. And even when that happened, it was often because Xie You-qing needed money. Whenever Xie You-qing asked for money, his father always just gave it to him, no questions asked.

Deep down, Xie You-qing really wanted to know what his father was thinking, but his father had never said a thing about that.

自己只能冷漠裝酷，假裝不想回答。

不過，現在最傷腦筋的是：該怎麼跟老爸開口說這件事？要他百忙中抽空一起去學校道歉，還要面對老師跟李昱維的家長，恐怕再平靜的爸爸也會忍不住唸上一陣子吧！

想到可能會被爸爸罵，或有可能被打一頓，謝佑青的心情說不出是害怕還是……期待？爸爸通常沒什麼時間，回家跟出門都是匆匆忙忙，能跟自己見到面的機會不是很多，更不用像電視上說的有什麼親子溝通或互動時間了。能讓爸爸好好看自己幾眼，聽自己說說話，其實很不容易。常常都是因為自己需要錢，開口說了，爸爸就大方打開錢包給，完全不會多問。

有時候，真的很想知道爸爸在想什麼，可惜他從來都不說。

Just then, the door opened and his father came in. Xie You-qing hurried to him and said, "Dad, my homeroom teacher needed you to go to school with me for a conference."

"For what?" his father asked wearily and only half-heartedly.

"Today, Li Yu-wei grabbed my new game console from me and dropped it on the floor, so I gave him a push," Xie You-qing answered quickly.

"Was that all?" his father asked deadpan.

"Ah, because...because the console seemed broken, so I was mad. I kicked him a few times and gave him a few punches," Xie You-qing said as he tried to steal glimpses of his father to fathom his mood and reaction.

"I see. Give me Li Yu-wei's home number. I will call them directly."

Xie You-qing wrote down the number and handed the slip of paper to his father.

開門聲響，爸爸回來了。謝佑青急忙走向老爸。「爸，我們導師要你找時間跟我去學校一趟。」

「有什麼事嗎？」爸爸一臉疲憊，好像有點心不在焉。

「今天李昱維搶我的新電動，還摔在地上。我就推了他一下。」謝佑青快速地說著。

「就這樣而已嗎？」爸爸臉上看不出情緒。

「嗯，因為……那台新的電動好像摔壞了，我很生氣，所以……踢了他幾腳，還有……揍了他幾拳。」謝佑青偷看著爸爸的反應，一邊回答。

「我知道了。你把李昱維家的電話給我，我直接打電話過去。」

謝佑青趕緊寫好李昱維家的電話後，把紙條交給老爸。

"I'll ask my assistant to take a gift box of something to his home to apologize and give them some money, so don't you worry about it," his father said as if nothing had even happened. "Anything else? If not, I need to get busy," his father said.

"Yes. One more thing. I was put in a timeout standing outside my classroom. A strange woman showed up and talked to me. She said that she was a fairy and her name was Green Fairy. She gave me a present, an elongated cloth bag," Xie You-qing said. He almost forgot to mention this to his father.

Before he could finish his thoughts, his father cut in and said, "Next time when you see a stranger on campus, tell your teacher or the school security guard. Don't accept any gift from strangers." Promptly, his father walked toward his study with that slip of paper.

Watching his father disappearing into the study, Xie You-qing felt a sense of loss. Perhaps in his father's mind, making money was his first priority, nothing else seemed to matter to him, not even when his own son had beaten people up.

「我會叫我助理帶禮盒去道歉跟賠錢。你不用擔心。」爸爸的表情好像什麼事都沒發生。「還有事嗎？沒事我就先去忙了。」

「對了！我今天上課在教室外面罰站的時候，還碰到一個奇怪的女生找我聊天，她說她是仙子，我可以叫她小綠。她還送我禮物，是一個長長扁扁的布包……」佑青差點把這件事給忘了，剛想起來就馬上跟爸爸說。

「下次校園裡再碰到奇怪的壞人，就跟你老師或學校警衛說一聲。不要亂收人家送的東西！」爸爸話都還沒聽完就打斷，拿著紙條就往書房走。

謝佑青看著爸爸的背影，心裡忽然有種失望跟失落的感覺。也許，爸爸的世界只有賺錢最重要吧。所以，兒子打人也沒什麼關係。

Quietly, Xie You-qing recalled his encounter with the Green Fairy. She appeared quite enthusiastic. She really didn't seem like a bad person at all. He had felt bored when he was standing outside his classroom, so it wasn't bad at all to have somebody there to talk to and kill time with.

Green Fairy said that even deity made mistakes. In fact that was why she had come to this world. She had inadvertently stepped on and crushed seven sprouts, and as a punishment she was sent to this temporal world to accomplish seven missions. She said that she knew that Xie You-qing had lost his mother at a young age and his father was always busy working.

Xie You-qing didn't really know how Green Fairy had emerged in front of him, how she disappeared, or why she gave him a present. But the most befuddling thing of all was what she said to him when she handed him the cloth bag: "This incense stick and this divine leaf will help you find the real reason why you fight."

"Do I even need a reason to fight?" Xie You-qing frowned and snorted.

默默回到自己的房間，謝佑青想著：小綠看起來很熱心，真的一點也不像壞人！上課時間被罰站在教室外面很無聊，有人陪著說說話，打發時間也不錯。

小綠告訴自己，就算是神仙有時也會不小心犯錯，像她就是因為踩壞了七株嫩苗，所以從天界來到人間。接著她說了一個奇怪的故事，是關於要完成七個任務的事。她還知道佑青從小就沒有媽媽，爸爸工作非常忙碌。

小綠從哪裡冒出來很奇怪，小綠怎樣消失也不明白，小綠為什麼要送自己禮物更是想不透，但是最奇怪的是，小綠送禮物布包時所講的話。

「透過這支天香與這片仙葉，你會找到你打架鬧事的真正原因。」

「還會有什麼原因？」謝佑青皺著眉冷冷地哼了一聲。

"It's just that annoying Li Yu-wei who loves to grab things from people and make trouble," Xie You-qing murmured to himself.

He casually opened the cloth bag. He stared at the slender incense stick. Two blurry characters were written on the incense. He thought if this incense stick knew a clue to why he fought, it might show "Li Yu-wei".

The divine leaf looked nothing out of the ordinary, just another leaf. Xie You-qing began to think. Could this have some bearing on some latest games? Could this be a free gift card, a game piece, or treasure? Xie You-qing anxiously grabbed the leaf and held it to a light to study it. The veins of the leaf seemed to loom with orange light.

Xie You-qing hesitated for a moment, unsure whether he should just return to playing familiar games to break some record or start following Green Fairy's instructions and light the incense stick. He decided to try the new thing. Perhaps he would waste time doing this, but that was okay. He had plenty of time on his hand.

「就是那個討人厭的李昱維愛搶別人的東西，愛找麻煩啦，無聊！」

謝佑青漫不經心地打開布包，瞪著那根細長的香，上面寫著看不清楚的兩個字。如果這支香藏有自己打架原因的線索，說不定香上寫的是李昱維的名字。

葉子看起來倒是很平凡，不過就是一片葉子而已。謝佑青搖頭晃腦想著，難道這跟什麼新出來的手遊或電玩有關？會不會是免費贈送的點數卡，還是遊戲道具或寶物？謝佑青充滿期待地用手抓起葉子朝著燈光研究，葉脈裡好像若隱若現透著橘色的光線。

謝佑青開始猶豫：現在該去玩熟悉的遊戲，打幾局電玩破個紀錄；還是要照著陌生人小綠教的方法，點燃天香？不如……嘗試看看新奇的事吧！浪費一點時間無所謂的，反正時間也很多。

He lit the incense stick. When smoke with a light aroma started rising, the leaf suddenly came to life, expanding and contracting as if breathing. Then orange light, bright like hot lava, started spreading in all directions into the veins of the leaf.

Xie You-qing found himself in a warm, orange atmosphere with air seeming to emit heat. Sounds like balloon popping came from somewhere not too distant. In the midst of flowing orange light, thin, transparent display screens with colorful videos and sounds appeared and floated in midair.

Xie You-qing was surprised when the first image to show up on the screens was that of his father, talking on the phone in the study, next to where Xie You-qing was.

"Mrs. Li, please don't blame my son, Xie You-qing. It's all my fault. I've been too busy to guide You-qing. I will take care of Yu-wei's medical expenses. I'm really sorry," his father was talking to Li Yu-wei's mother.

"Tomorrow at noon, my assistant will go to your home to formally apologize. She will give you the money for the medical expenses that you just mentioned. Thank you for your understanding."

當天香冒起一股淡淡香香的煙，葉子就像忽然有了生命一般，輕輕像呼吸般顫動起來。接著，像火山爆發滾燙岩漿般泉湧的橘光，開始朝葉脈與紋路的四面八方流動著。

謝佑青發現自己處在一種暖暖的橘色氛圍當中，連空氣都好像冒著熱度。不遠處偶爾傳來有點像氣球爆炸時音爆的聲音，像悶雷一樣嚇人。在緩慢流動的橘色流光裡，浮出一個個透明的薄幕，上面閃動著彩色的聲光與畫面。

沒想到在薄幕上第一個出現的畫面，竟然是正在隔壁書房講電話的老爸。

「李太太，請不要責怪我的兒子，是我的不對，我太忙，沒時間好好管教佑青，昱維的醫藥費我負責賠償。真是對不起。」

「明天中午我的助理會過去拜訪，正式道歉，妳說的醫藥費，她也會一起帶過去。謝謝妳的體諒。」

His father put down the phone and let out a long sigh as he feebly sat down in front of the desk.

He opened his briefcase, took out an old, slightly yellowed photo from his billfold, and looked at the photo. Xie You-qing recognized that was his mother. His father began to talk to the photo.

"Dear, I know that you'd know what to do if you were still alive."

"If you were faced with this, how would you handle it? I'm exhausted."

"You-qing seems to have entered the period of teenage rebellion. He has a short fuse. He either quarrels or fights with classmates, and he is addicted to video games. He doesn't like to do homework and he just ignores exams. He doesn't aspire to achieve things."

"I'm very busy and don't have time to guide him. I don't know what to say to him."

"Dear, if he wants money, I give him money. Whatever he wants to buy, I give him money. If he messes things up, I find a solution and pay the money for him. Isn't all this enough?"

放下電話的爸爸，長嘆了一口氣，很無力地坐在書桌前。

他打開公事包，拿出皮夾裡一張有點泛黃的舊照片，輕輕地對照片說：

「老婆，如果妳還在，一定知道該怎麼做，對吧！」

「老婆，如果是妳，妳會怎麼處理呢？我已經沒有力氣了。」

「佑青好像進入叛逆期，很容易生氣。在學校不是跟同學吵架就是打架，不然就是沉迷在電動玩具的遊戲裡。他不喜歡寫功課，也不管考試，也沒什麼上進心。」

「我很忙，沒時間管教，也不知道該怎麼跟他講。」

「老婆，他要錢，我就給他錢；他要買什麼，我通通都滿足他。他做錯事，我幫他解決、幫他賠錢。這樣還不夠嗎？」

"He's lost his mother. I really feel for him. I work hard to make money so that I may provide him with a comfortable and carefree life."

"Dear, whenever I see You-qing's eyes, I think of you. I miss you so much. That's why even when I get really mad at him, I don't have the heart to hit him or scold him."

Xie You-qing was a little shocked by this revelation. To him, his father, always bigger than life, could accomplish anything he had wanted to accomplish. Nothing had ever surprised him, saddened him, or made him mad. But now this giant of a man was at a total loss.

His father unlocked a drawer and took out a thick photo album. He opened the album, his eyes betraying his sadness. He looked deep in thought.

His father didn't usually let him into the study, and if he was allowed in, he was not allowed to move or examine anything. You-qing was very curious what's in the album; what were the photos that seemed so precious to his father?

「他沒有媽媽，已經夠可憐了。我努力賺錢，也是因為希望給他一個無憂無慮的生活。」

「老婆，我看到佑青的眼睛就想起妳，我真的很想妳。所以就算很生氣，但我怎麼打得下去？又怎麼忍心開口責罵呢？」

謝佑青有點吃驚。向來巨大的爸爸，向來無所不能的爸爸，向來什麼事都不會驚訝、不會難過、不會發脾氣的超淡定老爸，這個時候竟然手足無措。

爸爸打開鎖住的抽屜，拿出一本厚厚的相簿。然後眼神十分憂傷地打開相簿，陷入沉思。

平常，爸爸根本不准他沒事進書房，更不許他翻動任何東西。佑青很好奇相簿的內容。究竟是什麼寶貝珍貴照片，這麼吸引爸爸的注意？

One of the screens showed a photo of his father, then a little boy, and grandmother together; another screen flickered momentarily before showing that boy in a film.

The boy, standing beside a bed, was shaking a woman lying in the bed. "Mom, wake up! Open your eyes and wake up now," the boy shouted.

"Don't scare me. Wake up, wake up. Don't leave me, Mom!"

The boy looked quite young, possibly younger than Xie You-qing was now. Looking heavenward and kneeling on the ground, the boy said earnestly, "Heavenly Emperor, I beg you to save my mother and give her back to me, please."

Tears and grime covering his face, the boy just cried and wailed helplessly.
"What am I to do? What can I do now? Mom...."
Gradually, the sounds faded and the video vanished.

Soon shown on the screens was a photo of the boy, now a young man, and a young woman posing in front of a motor scooter. The young couple—Xie You-qing's parents—looked quite happy.

一張小時候爸爸跟奶奶合照的照片，在另一個薄幕上閃動著。忽然就變成了動態的影片，小時候的爸爸在床邊，很驚慌地搖著床上的人然後大叫。

「阿母，妳醒過來，妳趕快睜開眼睛醒過來啊！」

「妳不要嚇我，妳趕快醒過來啊！妳不要丟下我啦！」

爸爸看起來年紀很小，應該比現在的自己都還小，慌張地跪在地上求著老天爺。
「天公伯，我求你，救救我媽媽，把我媽媽還給我。求求你。」

那張布滿淚痕、髒兮兮的小臉皺著，哭號著，無助著。
「怎麼辦？我該怎麼辦啊？阿母……」
哭喊的泣音減弱了，畫面也慢慢消失。

又一張年輕的爸爸跟媽媽在摩托車前的合照，慢慢變成薄幕上的影片。

"Honey, this will be our home," pointing at the apartment building now under construction, the young man said to his wife.

"Wow! It's almost done. It's making progress every month. We're going to have our own home soon," Xie You-qing's mother said. Happiness and gentle smiles abounded on her face.

"That I was very poor as a child really has scared me ever since those days," he said to her. "I often had nothing to eat and I cried with an empty stomach. When I couldn't stand it anymore, I would just drink water, lots of it, like there's no tomorrow," he continued, a little bitterness in his eyes. "Therefore, I made up my mind to make money like mad so that my wife and children will never need to live a day of such miserable life."

"Don't you worry. It's okay if we don't have money." she said firmly with no room for rebuttal. "I'll be with you to live through bitterness and work hard for our goals. I will be with you through thick and thin. If we have to be hungry, we go through hunger together.

「老婆，這裡就是我們未來的家，現在還正在蓋。」爸爸意氣風發地指著面前正在興建的公寓。

「哇！快蓋好了！每一個月都有新的進度，我們快要有自己的家了！」媽媽滿臉幸福、溫柔地甜笑著。

「我從小窮怕了，常常因為沒飯吃、餓著肚子流淚。實在太餓了，就拚命灌白開水。」爸爸的眼神閃過一絲苦澀。「所以我下定決心要拚命賺錢，好讓我的老婆孩子一輩子都不用再過苦日子。」

「你不用擔心，沒錢也沒關係。」媽媽的語氣很堅決，不容許反駁。「我會陪著你一起吃苦，一起奮鬥，一起餓肚子也一起吃便當。」

Against a backdrop of splendidly colorful sky, the couple cuddled. It was beautiful and warm. Their image gradually faded from the screen and a new photo appeared.

It was a photo of Xie You-qing's mother in her patient bed in a hospital. His mother looked gentle but very sad. The photo began to turn into a video. Haggard but trying to show otherwise, Xie You-qing's father sat by her bed and held her hands tightly.

"Sweetheart, my darling," he began to weep uncontrollably.

"Darling, don't cry. I forbid you to cry. You will scare the fetus inside," pointing to her own bulging belly, she forced a smile and warned him. "It's my own decision to forgo chemotherapy and radiation treatments in order to protect the fetus. Please don't blame yourself, much less the fetus," she said.

"Let's love this child together, okay? Even when I'm gone one day, you must love him. Give him lots of love—yours as well as mine," she said with a smile, gently patting his hands.
"Remember to tell our child that his mother loves him very much, every minute of every day even I may not live to see him growing up."

兩個人互相依靠的身影在彩霞的映照裡，顯得無比美麗也無比溫馨。畫面漸漸隱沒。

再一張照片是媽媽在病房的照片。照片裡的媽媽眼神很溫柔，但是也很憂傷。照片開始動了起來，神情憔悴而強打起精神的爸爸靠在病床邊，發抖地伸手緊緊握住媽媽的手。

「老婆，老婆，老婆……」爸爸開始泣不成聲。

「親愛的，不要哭。也不許哭。你的哭聲會嚇到我肚裡的寶寶。」媽媽勉強地笑著警告。「為了孩子，不化療也不放射治療是我自己的選擇。你不要怪你自己，更不要怪孩子。」

「我們一起好好愛這個孩子好不好？就算有一天我不在了，你也要好好愛他，把我的愛一起給他。」媽媽面露微笑，輕輕拍著爸爸的手。「記得告訴孩子，媽媽雖然也許看不到他的成長了，也許沒辦法看到他長大變大人了，但是，媽媽很愛他。媽媽每一分鐘都很愛他。」

"I love our unborn son very much, too, but I also love you very much, dear," he sobbed out of control and held her hands tightly.

The screen slowly turned dark.

Suddenly, two thin, transparent screens popped up, side by side as if they were facing each other.

On one of the screens appeared Xie You-qing's father. He stood alone in front of the windows, looking out. The setting sun was painting a spectacular drawing of the world. He put down his notebook computer on which he was only halfway through making data-filled reports. He held a cup of steaming coffee in front of the windows and fell into deep thought.

On the other screen was none other than Xie You-qing. In front of him, a computer was blaring ear-piercing sounds while the computer screen was showing an ongoing online game emitting orange light. As if he had just thought of something, he got up and walked toward the study and then he stopped as if frozen, the computer game flickering in the background.

「我很愛這個還沒出生的兒子，可是，老婆我也很愛很愛妳啊。」

爸爸啜泣著緊握住媽媽的手不肯放開。畫面緩緩淡出。

接著忽然同時出現兩個薄幕，像是並排、更像是對望。

一個薄幕出現了爸爸站在窗前看向窗外的獨影。窗外是霞光萬丈的夕陽，爸爸放下桌上打了一半、充滿各種數據與報表的筆電，端著一杯冒著熱氣的咖啡，站在窗前沉浸在回憶與思緒裡。

另一個薄幕出現的是看起來有點冒失、有點莽撞的謝佑青，面前一台放送著刺耳的音效與聲響的電腦，畫面上是連線中刺激好玩的電玩遊戲，閃動著橘色的光芒。謝佑青像是忽然想起了什麼，站起身想向書房走去，然後定格似的停下腳步。背景裡的電玩遊戲兀自閃動。

"Don't you think that you and your father are very much alike?" asked Green Fairy, pointing at the two floating screens. She had just popped up in front of Xie You-qing.

"Are we? In what way, the eyes, noses, or mouths?" He stared at those screens to compare.

"You're both lonely and longing for love," Green Fairy said meaningfully. "You think your father loves money and does not love you. He works hard to make money so that he can support you to lead a comfortable life, just like that story of long hair and the comb , which is The Gift of the Magi written by O. Henry."

Xie You-qing was shocked, his eyes wide open, and he was speechless.

"The two of you love each other very much, but neither of you has a clue about how to talk to the other," Green Fairy said, shaking her head in sympathy.

"To spoil you, he works like mad to make money. However, he is remiss in his duty to guide you, so he feels sorry and does not dare to face the situation."

「你不覺得你跟爸爸其實很像？」小綠突然出現在面前，指著兩個薄幕。

「有像嗎？是眼睛、鼻子還是嘴巴？」謝佑青專注地凝視兩個薄幕，仔細地比較。

「同樣的，都很孤獨、很渴望被愛。」小綠意味深長地說。「你以為爸爸愛賺錢不愛自己，爸爸為了不讓你過苦日子所以努力賺錢。好像歐‧亨利寫的《麥琪的禮物》，就是那個「長髮與梳子」的故事喔！」

謝佑青表情很驚訝，睜大眼睛說不出話來。

「你跟你爸兩個人都很愛彼此，但卻又不懂得怎麼溝通。」小綠搖搖頭，十分同情。

「你爸爸因為溺愛孩子拚命努力賺錢，卻又因為疏忽孩子的管教，而愧疚不敢面對。」

"I know you well. You really are a good boy, but, not feeling loved, you become angry and you beat up other people. You hope that such behavior will attract your father to care about you and pay attention to you," Green Fairy said as she looked Xie You-qing in the eye. "Beating people is not courage; it's just brute force."

Xie You-qing had never before in his life heard such a direct description of himself, but she had really hit the nail on the head. She's spot on.

"Why don't you tell your father your true feelings for him? Don't second guess each other," Green Fairy said. "Telling the truth is real courage." That sounded like a winner to Xie You-qing.

"I know what to do now. Thanks, GF."

The ambient orange light disappeared. Xie You-qing found himself back in his room. He looked at the table. The divine leaf was still there, but it had begun to turn brown and wither on the edge. Only a little spark was left in the incense stick as it burned near its end.

「我懂你，真正的你是個好孩子，只是因為感受不到愛而憤怒打人，想以此引起爸爸的關心與注意。」小綠的眼睛直視謝佑青。「打人不是勇敢，打人只是蠻力。」

謝佑青第一次面對這麼直接的形容，有種一針見血、當頭棒喝的感覺。

「你為什麼不把你心中真正的感覺說出來，讓爸爸知道，而不是彼此互相猜測對方在想什麼。」小綠的建議聽起來很不錯。「這樣做才是勇敢！」

「我知道該怎麼做了，謝謝你小綠。」

四周的橘光不見了，謝佑青發現自己回到了房間。他看向書桌，葉子還在，但葉子的邊緣開始變黃枯萎；而天香只剩下一點點火星，微微地燃燒著。

Xie You-qing had a plan: He would write a letter to his father in just a moment in which he would express his gratitude and apologies to Dad. He would encourage Dad, and he would tell Dad that what he had always wanted could not be purchased with money. He had always wanted Dad's love and care. He would also say that he had always been very fortunate for having so much, a fact that had just now dawned on him.

He would also write a letter to Li Yu-wei. Though Li Yu-wei was wrong to grab the console from him, he should repent even more for beating him up.

Xie You-qing didn't know why, but after he had decided to apologize, he felt much relief as if a big boulder of agony had vacated from his mind and relief had immediately checked in to take up the space.

The incense stick had now completely burned up. A word appeared in its ashes: courage. The orange light in the veins of the divine leaf had also disappeared completely. Xie You-qing turned and saw Green Fairy becoming more transparent by the second.

謝佑青想著：等一下馬上要寫一封信給爸爸，內容是感謝、重點是道歉，還要鼓勵爸爸。他決定坦白告訴爸爸，自己要的從來不是錢跟那些花錢買到的東西，而是爸爸的關心。而自己原來擁有那麼多愛，卻一直身在福中不知道。

還有，要寫一封信給李昱維，雖然他搶東西是不對的行為；但是，自己暴力打人也有錯，更應該要懺悔。

不知道為什麼，決定説出道歉的同時，謝佑青心裡好像有一塊大石頭也終於放了下來。

天香燒完了。灰燼裡終於出現兩個字：勇氣。葉脈上橘色的流光已消失。謝佑青轉身看向小綠，小綠身影慢慢變淡。

Smile in her voice, Green Fairy said, "It takes a brave person to admit his mistakes and apologize sincerely for them. No coward can ever do those two things. You are a brave boy. You're so lovely. Thanks a lot for allowing me to accomplish my fourth mission. I'm rooting for you."

小綠滿意的笑聲朗朗傳來;「能面對自己的錯、真心道歉,從來不是弱者的行為,是需要很大的勇氣的。謝佑青,你真是個勇敢的孩子!太可愛了!謝啦!你讓我的第四個任務圓滿完成!為你加油!」

第五個任務
Mission Five

沒有看到的故事情節

A story untold

Wu Xin-jie habitually touched her chest to feel her heart, from the depth of which she could feel something flowing out—that uncomfortable, dull pressure in her chest that she just couldn't describe in words but was so familiar with. Doctors couldn't pinpoint what might have caused Wu Xin-jie's symptoms, which, like shadows, would manifest themselves only from time to time but not go away completely.

On this day, in fact right this moment, she was feeling that pressure again.

She had barely managed to put up with it long enough until she reached her secret base.

On the second floor of a convenience store not far from her home was her secret sanctuary, a nice place where she could spend some time after school before going home.

She wouldn't need to spend much money to enjoy some quality time there. At this place, she could come and go as she wished, and she would hardly be seen—and therefore bothered—by her classmates. Nobody there would pay any heed to her or give her a second look.

吳欣潔習慣性地觸摸安撫著心臟跳動的位置，那種說不出來的不舒服沉悶壓迫感，打從心臟的內部發送出來。明明檢查就找不到原因，這個毛病卻像糾纏的影子一樣神出鬼沒、不肯離開。

而今天、就是現在，那個毛病又再度作祟。

她好不容易忍著、撐著，來到了她的祕密基地。

離家不遠的便利商店二樓，一個可以打發放學後回家前時間的好地方。

花費不高、來去自由、遇到同學的機會不大、也沒人會注意別人在幹什麼。

There, she could do her homework, write her diary, read a novel, or simply stare blankly and snuggle herself deep in reverie— or veg out. Of course, she could also pass her time on her cell phone or settle herself down to quietly face her inner self.

It was a haven where she could escape from, if only for a little while, the nagging of her step-mother, a night market vendor, who would unceasingly order her to do this chore or that or to take care of her step-brother and step-sister. For Wu Xin-jie those two kids were rascals.

Presently as Wu Xin-jie stepped on the second floor in her haven, some people scattered in twos and threes. There were students from elementary and middle schools and a couple, who were whispering to decide where they would meet that night for a date.

Wu Xin-jie was glad that she could finally relax and let her aching heart return to normal. She walked toward a seat beside a big potted plant that offered some privacy.

Just then, a young student ran up the stairs, quick as a rocket, and smashed right into Wu Xu Xin-jie.

可以寫作業、可以寫日記、可以發呆看小說、可以手機上網打發時間、也可以安靜下來面對自己。

也是能暫時逃離在夜市擺攤的繼母，不停叨唸要她幫忙做家事、照顧兩個皮蛋弟妹的避風港。

二樓的座位三三兩兩的人散落坐著。有小學生也有中學生，還有一桌是情侶，正交頭接耳商量著接下來晚上要去哪裡約會。

想著終於可以鬆一口氣，讓放學時像被捏緊而悶痛的心臟慢慢恢復正常，吳欣潔準備選個靠近樓梯旁有大型盆栽的隱密好位子。

一個莽撞的小學生奔跑著上樓，像火箭一樣撞了過來。

The whole bottle of soft drink that he was drinking during his ascend to the second floor splashed on Wu Xin-jie's skirt.

"Why're you so rude?"
"Sorry, I didn't mean to."
"But you splashed your coke on my skirt!"
"Cuz I just didn't see you."
"Lousy luck today."

"Hey, I'm even worse than you. At least you're not hurt, but I have to buy another coke."

It seemed that the little boy was more pissed off by the event than was Wu Xin-jie. He rambled, his mouth pouted, and hurried— yes, running—down the stairs to buy himself another drink.

Wu Xin-jie looked at her soiled skirt, and the corners of her mouth drooped. She couldn't help that.

就這麼衰，正中紅心沒閃過，小男生迎面撞上吳欣潔。
他迫不及待邊走邊喝的飲料整罐灑了出來，潑在欣潔的
制服跟裙子上。

「啊！你怎麼這麼粗魯呢！」
「對不起啦！又不是故意的！」
「你把可樂都灑在我的衣服上了！」
「我就沒看到妳啊！就剛好嘛！」
「真倒楣！」

「我更衰好不好！妳又沒受傷，可是我可樂都沒了，害
我還要重買！」

小男生比吳欣潔更不高興，他嘀咕抱怨完那罐平白損失
的飲料，嘟著嘴又急忙跑下樓。

吳欣潔低頭看到衣服沾滿了黏黏甜甜的飲料，忍不住嘴
角下垂。

Then she took stock of her own life. Her dad was almost never at home. Her step-mother would use every trick in the book to get her to clean the house, do the laundry and the rest of household chores, and, of course, take care of the two rascals, those two pesky, filthy kids who loved to cry and throw fits. Her step-mother was squeezing every ounce of work out of Wu Xin-jie, who felt that she might as well be a servant and a babysitter all rolled into one, and a free one at that.

Wu Xin-jie was disgusted by the thought of those unpleasant things at home, which were like a thick layer of sticky slime growing on her skin that even soap and water could not remove. She touched her coke-soiled skirt. The soda had made it sticky, too, but at least she could wash away the sugary syrup.

"The kids are like aliens. I just don't know how to communicate with them," Wu Xin-jie thought.

"I definitely don't want to have my own kids later. Too much work."

"The heartache is bad enough. Now this thing on top."

"All these disgusting things would never happen to me if I had gone with Mom instead of Dad," she continued.

"It would have been wonderful if Mom had chosen me over Sis."

"I think Sis is having a much better life...."the thought of which seemed to have triggered the memory that would normally flash back only in her nightmare.

爸爸經常外出、老是不在家，繼母總是軟硬兼施地催促她幫忙做家事、打掃、洗衣服，還要照顧那兩個髒兮兮又愛哭愛跟的小鬼，簡直把自己當成不用付薪水的免費傭人兼免費保母；那種黏膩不舒服的感覺就像灑在身上的可樂，固執地沾在自己的皮膚上，就算用肥皂洗、卻怎麼都洗不乾淨。

「小孩根本是外星人，沒有辦法用語言溝通！」
「以後我一定不要養小孩，太麻煩了！」
「就已經不舒服了，還遇到這種事！」
「如果當初我跟的不是爸爸，而是媽媽的話，就不會遇到這些討厭的事了。」
「那個時候如果媽媽選擇帶走的是我，而不是妹妹，那該有多好……」
「妹妹現在應該過得很幸福吧！」
此時，在噩夢中才會出現的回憶，竟然又突然冒了出來。

A younger Wu Xin-jie was crying on a rainy night many years ago, pleading to her mother.

"Mom, can I go with you?"

"Take Sis and me with you, please. I'll take good care of her."

"I don't want to stay with Dad. I want to go with you."

"Sis is naughty, but I am good. Pick me."

"Mom, please. Don't leave me behind."

Mom, deadpan, said nothing and didn't even look at the teary Wu Xin-jie. Her only response to Wu Xin-jie's beseeching was a decisive shake of her head. Then she held Sis' little hand tightly, held up an umbrella, and walked away.

As Mom and Sis walked farther and farther away, Wu Xin-jie, without an umbrella, scrambled to look for them. She ran on the streets crying and shouting.

「媽媽，我也跟妳走好不好？」

下雨的夜晚，八年前的她還沒滿九歲。稚嫩的嗓音哭求著。

「妳把我跟妹妹一起都帶走，可不可以？我會好好照顧妹妹的。」

「我不想要跟爸爸，我要跟妳！」

「妹妹很皮，我很乖！我會幫忙照顧她。」

「媽媽，拜託啦，我也要跟妳走好不好？」

而媽媽臉上沒有表情也不說話，完全不看滿臉淚痕的吳欣潔，狠心地搖搖頭。然後緊緊牽著妹妹的小手，頭也不回地轉身撐傘離開。

看著媽媽與妹妹遠去的身影，吳欣潔急著想要馬上跟出去，卻被爸爸拉住。她掙扎半天才掙脫，傘也沒拿就直接衝到街上，焦急而瘋狂地奔跑尋找著，在馬路上大聲地哭喊著。

"Mom, please. I'll be a good girl."

"I swear I'll behave. I'll be better than Sis. You come back now."

"Mom, don't go. I beg you to stay."

"Mom, where are you?"

"Mom, I can't see you... Mom!"

Mom and Sis disappeared at an intersection. In panic, Wu Xin-jie, one foot tripping the other, fell on the street. The rain just kept coming down.

There wasn't time to worry about the pain and bleeding from her scraped knee; Xu Xin-jie sobbed on the dirty road, rain and tears leaving her face awash.

"Mom, Mom, don't leave me."

That was a very long night. Finally, Dad came. He picked her up and carried her home. She got a fever, and she couldn't stop having nightmares for days on end.

「媽媽，求求妳，我一定會很乖。」

「我發誓我真的會很乖，妳趕快回來……」

「媽媽不要走。求求妳不要走。」

「媽媽，妳們在哪裡？」

「媽媽，我找不到妳們……」

岔路口失去了她們倆的蹤影。吳欣潔恐懼而心急的腳步跟蹌了一下，一隻腳不小心絆到另一隻腳，就這麼摔倒在雨中。

顧不得膝蓋的破皮流血，忍著不敢喊疼，那個分不清臉上到底是雨水、汗水或淚水的自己一直嗚咽，蹲在骯髒的馬路上啜泣。

「媽媽，媽媽，不要丟下我……」

記得，那一夜好長，直到爸爸後來找了過來、把哭暈的自己抱回家；回家後開始發燒做噩夢，連續病了好幾天。

Wu Xin-jie came out of her memory. She asked herself, "Why am I thinking of these annoying things again? Haven't I tried to forget them all? Haven't I declared that I don't give a damn? But why am I still saddened by them?"

Her heart started to ache badly again.

"Heaven, what's wrong with it? Can it ever be cured? Ouch, it hurts." Wu Xin-jie pressed her heart. She couldn't breathe.

A gentle voice sounded. "Wu Xin-jie, are you all right?" It was from a woman. She had the bearing of a college student. "I'm Green Fairy," said the woman. "Do you need help?"

Wu Xin-jie's jaw dropped. Unable to speak, she just shook her head, took a deep breath and exhaled slowly. That seemed to have eased her heart pain.

吳欣潔眼神放空地想著：這些煩人煩心的事，幹嘛又想起來呢？我不是刻意忘掉了嗎？明明已經不在乎的，為什麼還會難過呢？

這個時候，心臟又開始狠狠抽痛了起來。

「天啊！我的心臟到底出了什麼問題？永遠沒辦法好嗎？好痛……好痛……」吳欣潔摀著心口低語，快要喘不過氣來了。

「吳同學，妳還好嗎？」看起來像大學生的氣質女生溫柔地關心著。「我是小綠。需要幫忙嗎？」

吳欣潔整張臉皺得像酸梅，因為無法說話慌忙搖搖頭，大口深深吸氣後慢慢吐氣，這才感覺舒服了一點。

"Heart pain, if caused by issues in the mind, generally doesn't respond well to medical treatment." Green Fairy said. The way she said it—filled with genuine care—seemed familiar to Wu Xin-jie. She thought of her long-lost mother.

"This kind of heart pain causes more suffering than most other diseases," Green Fairy said. "And it takes medicine of the mind to heal."

"I think this may be what you need the most," Green Fairy said, an almost divine spark flashing in her eyes. She handed a cloth bag to Wu Xin-jie.

"The fact that you and I have crossed paths indicates our affinity. This is a gift to you. I hope that it will be helpful." Green Fairy said.

Wu Xin-jie hurried home. She finished all her chores, made the two rascals to finish dinner, take showers, and watch TV for an hour, read a story to them, and finally tucked them in. She then did her homework. By the time she had finished homework, her step-mother had not returned home.

"An incense stick and a leaf. How could they be the magical treatment for my heart ache?" Wu Xin-jie murmured as she opened the cloth bag. She sniffed the incense stick, exuding a light, pleasant aroma. Could it be made from some Chinese medicine? The leaf exuded an even lighter, plantal aroma, and it gave a fine, hairy touch, almost a little velvety.

「心病，用一般的藥不容易治好。」小綠關懷的語氣有種熟悉感，讓吳欣潔想起了很久很久沒看到的母親。「心病，比起很多病，更讓人痛苦。」

「心病，往往要心藥才能醫。」

「我想，這可能就是妳最需要的。」小綠大大的眼睛閃動著靈光。她遞出了一個布包。「相遇就是有緣。這個禮物送妳。希望幫得上忙。」

回家忙完家事，吳欣潔盯著兩個皮蛋吃完飯洗好澡，然後等他們看完一小時電視、聽完自己講故事、兩個孩子都乖乖上床睡覺。欣潔寫完了功課，繼母還沒回家。

「一支香、一片葉子，這會是什麼神奇心藥？」
吳欣潔一邊打開布包、一邊碎唸著。她把香拿著靠近鼻子聞一聞，天香散發一股淡淡好聞的藥草香氣，這原料會不會是什麼中藥呢？葉子也散發出一種更淡的植物香氣，表面摸上去也有種纖細的茸毛觸感。

"Are these for aromatherapy?"

Now Wu Xin-jie remembered that a classmate had said that aromatherapy was interesting because her aunt was an aromatherapist, who had told the classmate that in aromatherapy, extracted essential oils were applied via massaging, bathing, or heated vapor. In other words, the aroma got into the human body through breathing or skin absorption to achieve the effects of relaxation and improved health. It was a natural therapy.

Wu Xin-jie felt that her own power to reason was probably right up there with the Detective Conan of the animation or Sherlock Holmes. In her judgment, that Green Fairy was probably an aromatherapist and the incense stick and the divine leaf were free samples for her to try them out.

"Green Fairy was just hoping that if I tried them, I would become a regular customer. Fat chance," Wu Xin-jie sneered. But she took a test drive anyway.

「這是什麼芳香療法吧？」

記得曾經聽同班的同學提過，說芳療很有趣。那位同學的阿姨是個芳療師，她說芳療就是藉由芳香植物所萃取出的精油，用按摩、泡澡、或是薰香等方式，經由呼吸道或皮膚吸收進入體內，來達到舒緩精神壓力與增進身體健康的一種自然療法。

吳欣潔覺得自己的推理能力應該跟柯南或福爾摩斯同等級厲害。她推斷那位小綠應該也是個芳療師，香和葉子都是贈送給自己試用的樣品。

「就等我一試成主顧嗎？我才不信呢！」

She lit the incense stick. Its smoke immediately strengthened its scent, and the divine leaf became less plant-like as red light—sanguine as blood—began to flow and spread out from the thickest veins to miniscule capillaries. In a short time, the divine leaf no longer remained flat as its edge slowly rolled up toward the center of the leaf. Lo and behold, the leaf had taken on the shape of a heart.

The heart-shaped thing grew larger and larger right in front of Wu Xin-jie's eyes. The sound of rhythmic heartbeats had now reached her ears. She was shocked when she realized that she was standing on the side of a dark-red path. Red light flowed all around the path. She couldn't help following the red light as it flowed steadily forward. She saw transparent thin screens floating in midair with colorful video images and audios.

She first saw her step-mother appearing on the screen. She was selling drinks in a night market.

點燃了天香,當香冒起煙的時候,香氣就更濃郁了。而葉子變得不像植物,紅色的流光就像血液一般,由最粗的葉脈主幹向四周細微的枝幹分支流動。葉片也不再扁平,四周向中心緩緩捲起,變成一個立體的心臟形狀。

吳欣潔看著越變越大的心臟影像,耳邊也響起規律的心臟脈動的聲音。她驚訝地發現自己站在暗紅色的道路邊,四周的紅光緩慢而規律地流動著,她情不自禁地跟著流光向前走,看到路邊浮出一個個透明的薄幕,上面閃動著彩色的聲光與畫面。

薄幕上第一個出現的畫面,是現在還在夜市擺攤賣飲料的繼母。

"Mrs. Wu, your drinks sold quite well today," said the woman who was tending the next stall. That woman was a chatterbox. "Business has been tough this year because of the COVID-19 pandemic. Customer traffic in the night market has taken a beating. Furthermore, how can you drink when you have a mask on? Luckily, infections have been well controlled lately, so business has picked up a little. We're in luck," Wu Xin-jie's step-mother replied. Her step-mother had always been enthusiastic and nice to people.

"It's been a while since your husband came to help. Where does he work now?" This woman likes to poke her nose into others' business.

"Don't mention it. He can't be relied upon. He doesn't care for the family, and I have no idea where he has been lately. He's just like his father. They both do not love their families. I don't want to think about him," her step-mother shrugged as if she couldn't care less.

"Don't you have several kids? That's a heavy load," that prying woman sounded sympathetic. Perhaps she was in the same boat as her step-mother.

「吳太太，妳今天飲料生意不錯哦！」隔壁攤的老闆娘很會聊天。

「今年生意很不好做，擔心新冠肺炎疫情啦！影響了逛夜市的人潮。戴上口罩也不好邊走邊喝飲料。還好最近防疫做得很不錯、生意有比較好，福氣啦！」繼母對別人總是很客氣，態度很熱情。

「好久沒看到妳老公來幫忙了，他最近在哪發財？」老闆娘看起來很愛打探消息。

「甭提他了！靠他是沒用的，不負責任不顧家，這幾天又不知道去哪裡混了！跟我公公一個樣，不戀家。我不管他了！」繼母聳聳肩，一臉不在意。

「妳不是有好幾個小孩嗎？這個擔子很重呢！」那位老闆娘可能處境相同，所以很同情。

"My husband sucks, but his daughter is his polar opposite. She's mature and she does as I ask her to. She's been a great helper. I work here to make money, and she takes care of my children after school," her step-mother, glowing, said to that woman. Wu Xin-jie was really shocked to hear her step-mother praise her behind her back.

"You're fortunate. You did a great job guiding her," that woman said with a good dose of jealousy.

"No, I haven't given her any guidance, and neither has my husband. Xin-jie is just a good girl," her step-mother continued to praise her. "Perhaps her mother did a fine job teaching her at a young age."

"Has her mother not come to visit her? Such a heartless woman," that woman said with a strong sense of justice in her voice.

Her step-mother hesitated at first but eventually said, "Her mother did come to me a few times. She said that she had saved some money and would like to take her back. But I didn't go along. Then she wanted to know how much money I wanted before I would let her take the child back."
"Where could I possibly find such a great helper?" her step-mother continued.
"My two little children cling to their big sister. They love her, and they spend more time with her than me. Can you believe that?"

「我那個老公不成材，不過他的女兒非常懂事、很乖，是我的好幫手。我負責賺錢，她上學回家就幫我顧家顧小孩。」沒想到繼母在背後竟然會說自己好話。

「好命哦！妳真會教！」那個老闆娘一臉羨慕。

「我沒教，欣潔自己是個好孩子！我老公什麼都不管的！」繼母很得意。「也許欣潔小時候，她媽媽就教得不錯吧！」

「孩子的媽媽沒來看孩子嗎？太狠心了吧！」老闆娘的表情正義感十足。

繼母遲疑了一下，開始解釋：「她媽媽是有來找過我幾次，說存了點錢想把孩子接回去。但是，我沒答應。她還問我要多少錢才肯把孩子還給她……」
「這麼好的幫手，我是要到哪裡去找啊？」
「兩個不懂事的小孩都很黏姊姊、很愛姊姊，跟姊姊相處的時間比跟我這當媽的還多！」

"True, I do often nag Xin-jie, but whatever good stuff I have got, I make sure that I give her a share."

"I have cared for her like she's my own biological daughter. If she gets sick, I am the only one taking her to the doctor."

"I've raised her for so long, and I've become bonded to her. I will not let her go."

"I don't care how much money her mother may offer, but I will not let Xin-jie leave. She's my priceless treasure. She's my daughter."

The images on the screen gradually faded out.

Wu Xin-jie was really, really surprised to find how deeply her step-mother had grown attached to her. Her step-mother didn't usually reveal her inner feelings.

"But wait. That's impossible. My mother did come to see me? When? How come I didn't know about that?" Wu Xin-jie shouted at the blank screen. Her heart was pumping almost violently, the ambient red light quickened, and the audio of heartbeats also sped up its rhythm.

Three new thin screens rose and waved with the musical rhythm of the videos that came on.

「我平常雖然會唸她，但是有什麼好東西一定有她一份。」

「我把她當自己親生的照顧，生病都是我帶去看醫生的。」

「養了這麼久，也有感情了，真的很捨不得！」

「給我再多的錢，我也不願意讓欣潔離開！我當她是我無價之寶，是我的女兒。」

薄幕上的聲音跟畫面慢慢消失。

吳欣潔很意外繼母對自己感情挺深的，平常繼母不太顯露這些心思。

「等一下！不可能！我媽有來找過我？什麼時候的事？我怎麼不知道？」看著已變空白的薄幕，吳欣潔的心臟劇烈跳動著，四周的紅色流光也迅速游動，遠處脈搏的跳動聲節奏也跟著加快。

三幅新升起的薄幕，跟著節奏舞動，一如戰場上的戰旗。

One screen began with an image that Wu Xin-jie had known only too well. She had replayed in her mind that scene again and again: Her mom tightly held her sister's hand, and the two of them walked quickly and heartlessly away. All Wu Xin-jie could see were their backs, they got smaller and smaller before vanishing altogether.

Another screen showed an equally familiar scene: her own terrified face looking in all directions for her mother and sister. Her knee was bleeding from a fall during her desperate chase after her mother and sister, who were by now nowhere to be seen. She yelled for her mother. She was in excruciating pain, but she wasn't sure whether the pain had come from her bleeding knee or her broken heart. She was befuddled and she blamed herself; she didn't understand what she had done wrong that might have caused her mother to go away with her sister but leave her behind.

Losing no time, the last screen then showed an animated film. A budding flower swayed in the rain. Thick thorns soon grew all around the flower to protect it.

有一幕是再熟悉也不過的身影。是媽媽緊緊牽著妹妹的
手，絕情地迅速離去的背影。越來越小的身影，終究化
成了一個句點。

另一幕自己也很清楚，那一張小臉四處驚恐地張望，愣
愣地看著膝蓋破皮流血咬牙忍痛，還拚命呼喚著消失了
身影的媽媽，不知是肉疼還是心更痛。小臉充滿迷惑與
自責，她不懂自己究竟做錯了什麼，為什麼媽媽選擇帶
走妹妹，而拋棄了自己。

最後一幕是擬真動畫。一朵稚嫩的小花，在風雨中搖晃。
然後，周圍開始長出粗壯的荊棘，帶著尖銳的刺，慢慢
罩住吞食了花朵、也保護住花朵。

Days and weeks passed; resentment and anger refused to remain suppressed, thus feeding the thorns to transform into barbed wire that tightly wrapped around the flower that now took on the shape of a heart.

Wu Xin-jie felt the return of her inextricable and unpredictable heart ache at the exact moment when the thorns started to change into barbed wire.

This time, her heart ached so much that she almost passed out. All her pent-up anger and resentment rose to the surface. Wu Xin-jie told herself: No matter how much the barbed wire might prick and bleed her heart and cause maddening pain, she would rather tough it out than cry and yell. She wanted the pain to teach her to forget and not give a damn.

"Mom did not love me. She loved only Sis," Wu Xin-jie reminded herself. "She plainly and cruelly deserted me!"

Just then Green Fairy asked her, "Are you sure that's the whole story? It's an abridged version, not the full episode." Green Fairy was standing in the shadow of red light where the road seemed particularly narrow because it was obstructed by piles of deserted garbage.

隨著時間過去，綿綿的恨意與憤怒再也控制不住，由荊棘轉變成有著尖刺而再也斬不斷的鐵絲，千絲萬縷纏繞著脆弱花朵般跳動的心臟。

就在荊棘開始變成鐵絲的那一刻起，吳欣潔開始了如影子般不時出現的莫名心痛。

這個時候，吳欣潔的心臟又劇烈地痛了起來，幾乎快昏了過去。憤怒與怨恨全都浮了上來。她告訴自己：寧可血肉模糊、痛到咬牙唇破流血也絕不再哭喊，就讓自己在痛苦中慢慢學會遺忘與不在乎。

「我媽一點也不愛我，她只愛我妹！」吳欣潔一字一句提醒自己。「她明明那個時候狠心地拋下我了！」

「妳確定妳看到的片段就是全部？那是精簡版，不是完整版。」小綠站在紅光的陰影處發聲，那一處的道路好像特別窄，周圍都是障礙物與丟棄的垃圾。

As Green Fairy walked out of the shadow, a wider and sharper screen came into view.

"Wu Xin-jie, switch to another angle to see the parts that you missed," Green Fairy said.

The screen showed a street corner not far from the scene on the previous screen—where young Wu Xin-jie had fallen and scraped her knee. A woman holding an even younger girl was hiding in that corner: She was crying with her hand covering her mouth. She was Wu Xin-jie's mother.

"Please forgive me, Xin-jie. I had no other choice," her mother said. "Currently I can't adequately support you and your sister at the same time. Wait for me. I will work hard to earn more money. When I've saved enough, I will come back to take you home with me. Then the three of us can live a better life together," her mother said.

"You're more mature and you are capable of taking care of yourself. That's why I chose your younger sister. She's more helpless, less mature, and less healthy than you."

小綠走了出來，她的身邊揚起一幅特別寬闊也更清晰的
薄幕。

「吳欣潔，現在請妳換一個角度，看看妳沒看到的部
分。」

薄幕上，那個哭泣蹲著的女孩身邊不遠的轉角，躲著一
個抱著更小的女孩、摀住嘴傷心痛哭的女人。

「原諒媽媽。媽媽真的是不得已的。」
「媽媽現在能力不夠，沒辦法同時養妳們兩個。等媽媽
多努力賺一點錢，或者多存一點錢，到時候我會把妳接
過來，我們一家三口好好幸福過日子。」

「妳比較成熟懂事、可以照顧自己，所以我帶走了更無
助、更不懂事、身體比較不好的妹妹。」

"Be a good girl and don't be so sad. Mom really loves you."

"You're my dear baby. I couldn't bear to leave you. It was a very painful decision that I had to make, and I'm already regretting it. I'm in more pain than anybody else."

"The two of you are my children. It pains me to leave either of you."

The woman was crying, but she bit her lips so as not to make a noise and attract attention. She bit so hard that her lips bled.

In the twilight, Green Fairy was sad too.

"Sometimes people make decisions to which there are no alternatives. They just can't help it even though they know full well that their choices will not be understood, much less accepted."

Wu Xin-jie looked at her mother on the thin screen. Now she really got what her step-mother had said, and now she could appreciate the dilemma that her mother was facing in choosing from the available options.

「妳要聽話，不要傷心，媽媽真的很愛妳。」
「妳是媽媽的心肝寶貝，媽媽非常捨不得妳。必須做選擇，讓媽媽很痛苦，也很後悔，我比任何人都苦啊！」

「都是我的孩子，要放下誰我都很痛……」
哭泣的女人哭得很傷心，緊緊咬住嘴唇不敢哭太大聲，嘴唇都被咬破流出血來。

看著薄幕的小綠，神情很哀戚。

「有的時候，有的選擇是不得不做的。不管選了什麼，都很無奈不得已、也很難被理解被認同。」

吳欣潔看著薄幕上脆弱的媽媽。她真正懂了繼母所說的話，也感受得到當時母親的為難。

"Perhaps you are not turned off by children in general, but rather you have been haunted all along by yourself—that little helpless girl crying on the road misunderstanding that her mother had abandoned her," Green Fairy offered a theory.

"Because you cannot, dare not face that reality, so you have chosen not to face it," Green Fairy said. Her voice sounded like a distant morning bell to wake people up for the day.

In tears, Wu Xin-jie turned to the animation on the screen. Right before her teary eyes the barbed wire that had so inextricably constricted the heart for so long began to loosen. Inch by inch, the barbed wire transformed back to thorns, and the thorns back to dirt, the dirt went back to the earth.

Right at this moment Wu Xin-jie's heart stopped aching.

The shadowy corner from which Green Fairy had just stepped out moments before also began to change. All the shadows disappeared, as did all the piles of deserted garbage. The road now became wide and unobstructed.

「也許，妳不是討厭小孩，而只是討厭當年那個因為誤會媽媽拋棄了自己，獨自哭泣又不知道怎麼辦的妳！」

「因為無法面對、不敢面對、所以乾脆不面對！」
小綠的聲音有點像遠處傳來的暮鼓晨鐘。

吳欣潔含淚看向那個薄幕上的動畫，那個被鐵絲環繞囚禁住的心臟，外圍的帶刺鐵絲漸漸鬆脫、一寸一寸變回荊棘，荊棘慢慢變成泥土後，回歸到地裡。

此時此刻，吳欣潔的心臟，終於停止了不時的抽痛。

當小綠身後陰暗的角落亮起，陰影消失了，那些障礙物與垃圾也跟著不見，路面立刻顯得很寬廣通暢。

The red light gradually faded. Wu Xin-jie found herself in her own room. The two rascals were sleeping tight like angels.

Green Fairy gently patted Wu Xin-jie's hands.

"Now you know. Your mother and step-mother love you in their own way; your brother and sister admire you," Green Fairy said. "One more thing, you guessed wrong. I'm Green Fairy from heaven, not an aromatherapist in this temporal world."

Wu Xin-jie blushed.

"I really appreciate your help, GF," Wu Xin-jie said, a little shy, confident, and bright. "You've helped me unshackle my mind."

"I helped you see the whole truth," Green Fairy said. "You and you alone hold the key to extricating yourself from the grip of your mental pains."

Green Fairy was overjoyed. She was happy to see that the worrisome, dark shadow in Wu Xin-jie's face was now totally gone.

紅光慢慢遠去。吳欣潔發現自己還是在房間裡，兩個小皮蛋像小天使般睡得很香甜。

面前的小綠輕柔地拍著吳欣潔的手安慰著。

「現在妳知道了吧！妳的母親跟繼母是以不同的方式愛著妳，妳弟弟妹妹也都很崇拜妳呢！」
「還有啊，妳猜錯了，我是來自天界的綠葉仙子，不是人間的芳療師！」

吳欣潔的臉忍不住紅了起來。

「真的很謝謝妳！小綠。」吳欣潔的表情害羞中帶點自信與開朗。「因為妳，我才有機會解開了我的心結。」

「我只是讓妳看到事情的全部真相。化解心結的力量與關鍵，在妳自己。」

小綠很高興，吳欣潔臉上曾經讓人心疼擔憂的陰暗已經消失了。

"BTW, both your mother and step-mother love you very much. If you could choose only one, who would that be?" Green Fairy decided to tease her principal.

"That kind of choices is only for little kids to make. I love them both, and I want them both. When I am more financially able, I'll take care of them both," said Wu Xin-jie a little mischievously.

"Haha, I like that," Green Fairy said, quite satisfied by her reply. "Your step-mother will be home soon. I should go now," Green Fairy said as she began to fade out.
"Remember to check the incense stick for its message to you."

The incense stick had now totally burned up. A message had emerged to the top of its ashes: Thoughtfulness.

"Wu Xin-jie, please remember that there are no knots that can't be untied if you are willing to let go of your grievances. As long as you let go of the mental trash that has encumbered you, you can experience real happiness. Best of luck."

「對了！妳的母親跟妳的繼母都很愛妳，如果要妳只能選一個，妳會選誰？」小綠決定逗一下吳欣潔。

「只有小孩子才做選擇，我兩個都愛、兩個都要！等我有能力，我兩位都會孝順！」吳欣潔的表情也有點調皮。

「哈哈！很好！我喜歡！」小綠很滿意這個回答。身形也開始模糊。
「妳繼母快要回來了，我也該離開了！」
「記得看天香，有妳的短訊。」

天香燒完的灰燼裡出現兩個字：體諒。

小綠的聲音幽幽傳來：「吳欣潔，記得哦，沒有解不開的心結，只有不肯放開的怨念，只要妳放下掛礙的垃圾，就能體會真正的快樂呢。福氣啦！」

第六個任務
Mission Six

大人也會犯錯
A slap in the face

"Let's visit your father after school."

"Whatever went wrong, he is your dad."

"Are you going? It's now or never."

"Don't do things now that you may regret later."

"Be good. Don't be headstrong."

Guo Yan-zhi lay in bed with all of his limbs spread out. This was the most comfortable and his favorite posture in bed. In this pose, he could relax beginning from the tips of his fingers and toes toward the middle of the body, think of nothing, and feel his whole body lighter and lighter and his mind emptier and emptier as if he were floating in water or walking weightlessly in space. All his worries and troubles, now out of his mind, could wait till tomorrow or the day after countless tomorrows.

Usually, this had put him to sleep in short order, but oddly not today.

「晚上放學後，你跟我一起去看看你爸。」

「不論怎樣，就算過去發生了那些事，他都是你爸爸。」

「你再不去，以後說不定就再也沒機會去了。」

「不要做讓自己以後會後悔的選擇。」

「不要倔強了！聽話。」

郭彥志懶洋洋地呈大字型躺在床上。這是他最喜歡也最習慣的舒服姿勢。身體的四肢從手指與腳趾開始放鬆、腦袋瓜試著什麼也不想、身子越來越輕、思緒越來越空。逐漸，身體與心靈就好像漂浮在水面上、不然就是在無重力的太空中流浪。天大的煩惱，都留給明天、或明天的明天、或無數個明天以後的明天，再來傷腦筋。

通常，這很有效。幾分鐘後就可以進入睡眠中。可是，現在卻怎麼樣也睡不著。

He could think of only one reason: He had refused to go with his mother to see his father at the intensive care unit of a hospital yesterday, when the hospital notified his mother to hurry back to the hospital. She asked Guo Yan-zhi to go with her. After sleeping on the request all night, he couldn't make up his mind. But when the morning came, he told her that he couldn't go to the hospital because he wasn't feeling well.

"I didn't sleep well last night because I had a nightmare. I woke up feeling a chill and weakness. I am dizzy," he lied to his mother.

"Are you really sick or you just don't want to see your father?" she asked.
"But you aren't warm", she felt his forehead. "How about going to the hospital for an examination?"

Guo Yan-zhi played the role he had just invented for himself. He shook his head infirmly. "I'm terribly dizzy. Perhaps going back to sleep will help," he said feebly.

可能因為，他拒絕陪媽媽去醫院的加護病房探望父親。昨天晚上醫院通知媽媽，要媽媽趕緊去探視住在加護病房的爸爸。媽媽苦口婆心想要說服郭彥志，找時間一起去探病。郭彥志想了一夜，還是無法下定決心。今天早上他就騙了媽媽，說自己身體不舒服。

「昨天晚上做了惡夢沒睡好，今天起床有點發燒，覺得沒什麼力氣、頭一直轉、有點昏。」

「你是真的不舒服？還是根本不想去看你爸？好像沒怎麼燒……」媽媽摸了摸他的頭，擔心的神情中有點疑問跟試探的味道。「要不要順便去醫院掛號看門診、找醫生檢查一下？會不會是著涼了？還是感冒？」

郭彥志發現自己也挺會演戲的，馬上虛弱地搖頭、擺出一臉的疲憊、兩眼無神、全身都軟趴趴的樣子。
「好昏！我再多睡一下，應該就會好一點。」

"There are more germs in the hospital, so it's better that you stay at home," she said hesitantly.

"Rest and drink lots of water, and you should get better," she told him. "I'll call your teacher to ask for a day off for you. We can visit your father when you get better...if that's not too late."

She quickly cooked some porridge and said to him before she went out the door, "The regular visiting hours at the hospital are 6:00 a.m. till 10:00 p.m., but they're different at the ICU: 11:00 a.m. to noon, 2:00 to 3:00 in the afternoon, and 7:30 to 8:30 in the evening. Got that? You rest well at home. I'll slip out between my cleaning jobs to see your father, so I'll be home later than usual tonight."

Guo Yan-zhi unexpectedly got a day off school, but he couldn't find any reason to feel good about it. He ate the porridge for breakfast and felt thoroughly bored afterward. He couldn't find the energy to study, so he lay in bed, not feeling sleepy at all.
He shut his eyes anyway. Then things about his father, big and little, overflowed in his memory banks.

Very late one night, Mom was sleeping on a sofa. Dad still wasn't home. Mom had been on that sofa all night waiting for him.

「醫院裡病菌比較多，你不去也好。」媽媽有點猶豫。

「多休息、多喝水、應該就會好了。」

「好吧！那我先幫你跟老師請假。你今天在家裡休息。等身體好一點，我再帶你去探望。希望……來得及……」

媽媽匆匆忙忙煮好稀飯後出門，一邊叮嚀：「醫院的一般病房探病時間是：早上六點到晚上十點；加護病房探病時間不一樣，是上午十一點到十二點、下午兩點到三點、晚上七點半到八點半。不要搞錯了。你在家好好休息。媽媽趁打掃空檔去看爸爸，會晚一點回家。」

郭彥志無意中得到一天在家休息的時間，可是，他卻高興不起來。吃完稀飯很無聊，也沒辦法專心看書。乾脆就像這樣躺在床上，卻一點睡意也沒有。

一閉上眼睛，就會想起關於爸爸大大小小的事。

以前爸爸遲遲晚歸，甚至到快天亮才回家，而媽媽在沙發上等到睡著。

Dad finally came back. "Why don't you sleep in our room? Aren't you cold in the living room?" he asked Mom.

"Without seeing you home, I can't sleep well. I worry that you may be caught in an accident," Mom said.

"Hush! Can you ever stop cursing and start saying something nice?" Dad shouted. "I've been unable to accomplish anything I've attempted; even in gambling, I've lost. It's all because of your cursing."

"Give me ten gamblers, and I'll give you nine losers. Please stop gambling. Just see how much gambling debts you've piled up. Creditors have knocked on our doors. Some said that they would throw paint on our house if you don't pay them back. This would scare Yan-zhi," Mom countered.

"You're still cursing! I just told you to stop, and you just keep on nagging. That's enough," Dad shot back loudly, half drunk and raising his arm as if ready to slap Mom.

「妳幹嘛要睡不進房間睡，偏偏睡在客廳，不冷嗎？」

「沒看到你回家我不放心。怕你在外面出了什麼意外。」

「呸呸呸！妳嘴巴裡能不能說出幾句好話！我都是被妳詛咒，才會搞得做什麼都不順！連摸個牌也會輸！」

「十賭九輸！不要再賭了，你欠的錢越來越多，債主都上門來討，還說要來潑漆，會嚇壞彥志的！」

「妳還說！叫妳不要說，妳偏偏說個不停！煩死了！」帶著酒意的爸爸講話很大聲。他一邊吼叫一邊將手臂高高舉起，差一點就要對著媽媽揮了下去。

"I went back to gambling to win my money back, don't you understand? So, why are you saying all the nonsense? You're such a jinx," Dad continued. His raised arm slapped down, away from Mom, sweeping the bowls, plates, and cups off the dining table and onto the polished-pebble floor.

The ensuring ear-piercing noise from breaking china sacred Mom into silence.

"I'm exhausted, so you be quiet. I'm going to bed," Dad, face ashen, said as he careened.

Mom watched him walking away, tears streaming silently down her face.

From behind a door, Guo Yan-zhi restlessly watched his parents' sharp exchanges. He had been awoken by the noise of his father's return, so he slipped behind the door. He was concerned that his father might hurt his mother, whose tears, like an acidic fluid, had gradually eroded Guo Yan-zhi's love for his father.

「我是要去翻本，把錢賺回來，妳懂不懂啊！吵什麼吵？真是烏鴉嘴！」爸爸的手臂轉了方向，把餐桌上的杯子盤子碗通通掃到磨石子地磚上。

刺耳的破碎聲讓媽媽驚訝皺眉、嚇得不敢再說話。

「我很累了！妳安靜點！我去睡覺了！」爸爸臉色鐵青，搖晃著腳步回房間。

媽媽看向著爸爸的背影，眼淚無聲地一顆顆滑落。

被爸爸回家大吵大鬧聲驚醒的郭彥志，躲在門後面緊張偷聽。他很怕爸爸不小心就會擦槍走火，出手傷到媽媽。而媽媽的眼淚，像酸性液體一般，一點一滴慢慢侵蝕了郭彥志愛爸爸的心。

His father, once drunk, would become a senseless beast that was powerful and highly destructive and damaging. Every time Guo Yan-zhi saw his mother cleaning up broken things at home, he knew that chances were good that his father had gotten drunk again and made a mess.

Guo Yan-zhi thought helplessly: Dad just can't help gambling, piling on his mountain of debt. Mom has been thoroughly heartbroken for too long. They are constantly fighting, and they may end up in a divorce.

Guo Yan-zhi remembered one evening. His father came home smelling like alcohol, stuttering, and very irritable. His mother appeared to try to restore her composure from crying not long before. She told his father that someone had come to the house in the evening demanding repayments.

"To support our family, I've sold all my valuable belongings including my dowry and used up all the money I have been able to find, such as my savings before I married you, the money I had borrowed from relatives and my parents. On top of that, you recently lost your job," his mother said.

喝醉了酒的爸爸，會變成無法講道理的野獸。破壞力很強，傷害性也很高。每次看到媽媽急著收拾破破爛爛的物品，郭彥志就猜到：可能是爸爸又鬧事了。

他無奈地想著：爸爸控制不住愛賭，越欠越多的債讓媽媽傷透了心，兩個人又爭吵不斷，最後可能會走上離婚這條路。

記得那一天傍晚，爸爸回家時渾身酒氣、講話有點大舌頭、態度很火爆。媽媽滿臉愁容，好像剛哭過，鼻音很重地說傍晚有人來討債。

「我能賣的都賣光了，我當初嫁過來的嫁妝、我結婚前存的私房錢、我能借錢的朋友親戚也都借完了、我還跑回去娘家借錢，加上你最近又失業……」

"Are you finished talking?" his father yelled back, looking so agitated that he would soon erupt like a volcano.

"We've exhausted all we've got. How can I keep silent?" Mom felt that she had been woefully mistreated and wronged.

"You deserve it. I warned you before; if you say one more word, I'll...." Before he could finish the sentence, he raised his arm, taking aim at her.

"Don't hit Mom!" Guo Yan-zhi dashed forward just in the nick of time for his face to catch a slap from his father's rapidly descending arm.

Guo Yan-zhi couldn't recall exactly what had happened after the slap. As it turned out, his father was in shock; almost fully awake by now, he stared at his palm. His mother pushed Guo Yan-zhi back to his own room, and his parents went into their bedroom and closed the door behind them. There weren't any loud arguments this time. That's out of the ordinary. The next day, they decided to divorce.

「妳夠了沒有？到底有完沒完啊？」爸爸一臉不耐煩，就像快要噴發的活火山。

「家裡快要山窮水盡了，我怎麼能不說？」媽媽很委屈。

「我警告妳，是妳自己活該！妳再說我就……」爸爸高舉的手臂這次好像瞄準了媽媽的臉。

「不要打媽媽！」衝過來擋在媽媽前面的郭彥志，一點也沒考慮自己會不會受傷。
「啪！」的一聲，那一個熱辣辣的巴掌，就這麼落在郭彥志的臉上！

後面接著發生的事情，郭彥志已經記不太清楚了。爸爸瞪著他自己的手、呆住驚訝的表情，好像酒已經醒了一大半。媽媽半拉半推地要郭彥志回他自己的房間。然後爸媽兩個人回到主臥室關起房門說話。隔天，爸爸媽媽就決定離婚。

Subconsciously, Guo Yan-zhi believed that he himself had led to their divorce. This thought had since haunted him and he didn't even know it. This thought had consequently influenced his behavior after his parents' divorce.

After their divorce, Guo Yan-zhi lived with his mother. At times his mother would tell him that his father had requested a visitation to him. He had always just turned it down out of hand.

"What's the point of meeting? No, I don't want to see him," Guo Yan-zhi snapped.

"He's your dad, no matter what. Nobody can change that fact," his mother said.

"I don't want to meet him unless he stops drinking, gambling, hitting people, and calling people names," Guo Yan-zhi said.

"Give him a little time. He said that he would quit these bad habits."

"I'll believe it when I see it, so let's cross the bridge when we come to it."

郭彥志潛藏在心中真正的憂慮，是很害怕父母離婚的導火線是自己害的。

所以，每一次由媽媽轉達爸爸要求跟兒子會面，郭彥志總是冷冷地直接拒絕。

「有什麼好見的？不想見！」

「不管怎樣，他總是你爸！這是改變不了的。」

「除非他不再喝酒、不再賭博、不再打人、亂罵人！」

「給他一點時間吧！他說了會改會戒的！」

「那就等爸爸都改好了再說吧！」

Every time his father asked his mother to relay his wish to meet Guo Yan-zhi, Guo Yan-zhi just flatly declined. This routine was repeated over and over, pushing the time the two of them would meet back further and further. Now the world of Guo Yan-zhi centered on his mother alone. She worked hard as a cleaning lady for a paltry pay by the hour, and she worked hard to take care of her son as a mother and a father. The two of them depended on each other.

Were it not for that slap from his father, perhaps, just perhaps, the three of them would still be together today. Were it not for his father's alcoholism, addiction to gambling, and debts, his mother would not need to work quite so hard and shed so many tears. Were it not for his father, their world would be whole. Even so, Guo Yan-zhi could not put his father, now in critical condition at the ICU, out of his mind. He was pulled by these two opposing forces, and he couldn't make up his mind whether he should pay his father a visit.

Finally Guo Yan-zhi decided to go to the hospital without announcing his arrival and then he would play by ear.

就這樣一次一次拒絕，一次一次把會面時間往後延。郭彥志的生活中只留下媽媽。媽媽要忙著幫人打掃的鐘點工作、又要忙著照顧彥志。身兼父親與母親兩職的媽媽，跟彥志兩個人相依為命。

如果不是因為爸爸的那一巴掌，也許全家人還在一起；如果不是爸爸酗酒愛賭又欠債，媽媽不用那麼辛苦、也不必流那麼多眼淚；如果不是爸爸，世界是完整的。但他也不捨病痛中的爸爸，苦惱著不知道究竟該不該去探望。

「萬一爸爸真的病得很嚴重，怎麼辦？」郭彥志決定偷偷去醫院看看再說。

He put on a face mask before walking into the hospital. He paced in a long hall, but after a few laps he still couldn't summon up enough courage to step into the ICU.

"Should I or should I not go in to see Dad?" Guo Yan-zhi asked out loud, unintentionally.

"It's very hard to make a decision, right?" said a genteel woman as she walked toward him. "Guo Yan-zhi, you may observe more and think about it more before you decide."

"But I don't have much time," Guo Yan-zhi said anxiously.

"Yes, there is still time, but don't miss it," the mysterious woman said, handing him a cloth bag. "This will help you make the best decision."

"I am Green Fairy. You can just call me GF. I hope I can help you," she introduced herself.

他戴著口罩，在醫院裡有點陰暗的長廊徘徊了很久，來回踱步很多次，還是鼓不起勇氣，無法走進去加護病房探病。

「怎麼辦？我到底該不該進去看他？」郭彥志不小心大聲喊了出來。

「要做決定，很不容易對不對？」一個很有氣質的女生朝他靠近。「郭彥志，你如果不知道該怎麼做，可以先多觀察、多思考一下再決定。」

「可是，我沒多少時間了！」郭彥志很苦惱。

「時間一定有！只怕錯過機會！」神祕兮兮的女生將布包交給他。「這會幫助你做出最好的決定。」

「我是小綠，希望能幫到你。」

Guo Yan-zhi went home without seeing his father.

At home, he felt lost, so he opened the cloth bag, guessing that he would find a bookmark with some inspirational poems or messages, perhaps something like "there's no faulty parents under the sun," "filial piety is the foundation of a sound family," "when the child wants to take care of his parent, the parent is already gone," or some such "Golden Rule." He only vaguely remembered that Green Fairy had said something about an incense stick, a divine leaf, and magical power. He had only listened absent-mindedly.

"Sure enough, it's an incense stick and a divine leaf," he said to himself.

His room was still quite bright at the time, so he drew in the curtains to block out the light. Since he didn't know what else to do, he decided to give GF's suggestion a try—as a last-ditch effort to solve his problems. He lit the incense stick. As smoke rose, the divine leaf began to shake and emit bundles of blue rays in all directions. The walls in his room receded rapidly. The scent of sea water abounded in the damp air; the roars of the Yellow River surging onward, much like that of ten thousand horses galloping, filled the ear. The divine leaf, like the Transformers, had now elongated, widened, and rhythmically transformed into a small boat.

回到家，郭彥志感覺很落寞。他打開布包，他猜裡面可能是一張籤詩或是寫了勵志文字的書籤。也許是「天下無不是的父母」、「孝順為齊家之本」、「樹欲靜而風不止，子欲養而親不待」之類的金玉良言。他記得小綠後來有說了一些關於什麼天香、什麼仙葉、還有魔法的話，可是自己並沒有專心注意聽。

「竟然真的是一支香、跟一片葉子！」

郭彥志看看自己的房間光線還挺明亮，於是伸手拉上窗簾遮光。死馬當活馬醫，就來試試小綠的禮物吧。當天香被點燃、直直冒煙的時候，那片葉子忽然動了起來，由中間向周圍四面八方，不斷投射出一片又一片立體的藍色光芒，房間四周的牆開始迅速往後退，空氣中透著一股潮濕海水的味道，耳朵也傳來一陣又一陣萬馬奔騰的浪濤聲。葉片逐漸像電影裡的變型金剛一樣變長變寬，以有韻律感的節奏變成一條小船的模樣。

What really made Guo Yan-zhi's jaw drop was that he himself was now in that boat as it floated in the boundless sea. The ceiling in his room had already disappeared when he wasn't watching. Therefore, the boat was now drifting under a clear, cloudless blue sky.

The sea was still; the boat was slow-moving. It had neither power nor direction; it just went with ocean currents.

Guo Yan-zhi lay in the boat with his limbs spread out. He leisurely stared at the blue sky.
A blue ray flashed across the sky and ushered in many thin transparent display screens showing colorful videos and audios.

The first image to show up was that of Guo Yan-zhi's father, about seven years old. He looked a little like Guo Yan-zhi. The boy, nose running, neck tightened, fingers trembling, was standing there nervously and motionlessly.

郭彥志驚訝得合不攏嘴，他發現自己竟然置身在一葉小舟裡，而小舟正漂流在雲煙瀰漫、廣闊無邊的大海上。房間的天花板也不知道什麼時間不見了，變成了乾乾淨淨，萬里無雲的藍天。

海面很平靜，小舟移動非常緩慢。沒有動力、也沒有方向，就順著洋流漂流著。

郭彥志用自己最熟悉的姿勢，呈大字型躺在小舟上，悠閒地看著藍天。
潔淨的天空閃過一道藍光，浮出一個個透明的薄幕，上面閃動著彩色的聲光與畫面。

出現了第一個畫面，是長相跟自己有幾分神似的爸爸，大概只有六七歲的樣子。攟著透明的鼻涕，縮著脖子，緊張地顫動著手指，乖乖立正站好，不敢亂動。

"Were you born to put me in lousy luck? I've been in bad luck ever since your birth. Stop crying, otherwise I'll smack you," said a man to the boy. The man with a big stick in one hand and a liquor bottle in the other would be Guo Yan-zhi's grandfather. "You bustard, how dare you to steal!" the man continued.

"Dad, I didn't steal it. I didn't," the boy shook his head furiously.

"Still won't tell the truth? Have a few more sticks," the man said, hitting his son with the stick. Through the first few hits, the boy just bit his lips tightly without moaning, but the excruciating pain overwhelmed him and he wailed uncontrollably through subsequent strikes.

"Stop crying. It's precisely your crying that has depleted my luck in rolling dice," the man, too, was out of control. "I'll beat you till you stop crying!" He struck the liquor bottle in his hand against the wall. A piercing sound of breakage blared upon impact.

The boy trembled in unspeakable fear.

「生了你這個討債鬼，我就一路走衰運！哭！你再哭！你敢再哭我就扁你！」一手拿著大棍子、一手拎著酒瓶的男人應該是年輕時的祖父。「你這個臭小鬼，還敢偷東西！」

「爸爸，我真的沒有偷！我沒有！」小男孩的頭搖得像波浪鼓一樣猛烈。

「不老實，不老實的話再多打幾下！」當棍子落在小男孩的身上，起初幾下，小男孩還撐著咬牙，忍住不哭。後來實在是太痛了，小男孩忍不住嚎啕大哭起來。

「還哭！就是你哭！把我賭骰子的運氣全部哭光光！」「再哭！就揍到你哭不出來！」酒瓶往旁邊一砸，發出巨大的碎裂聲音。

小男孩哭到鼻涕又流了出來也沒擦，嚇到全身都在顫抖。

"Don't hit the child. If he said he didn't steal, then he didn't!" said the man's wife, Guo Yan-zhi's grandma.

"If it wasn't him, then it must be you who stole it. Good, I'll beat you up, too." The drunk man looked quite hideous.

The screen faded out among the man's strikes and the crying of the woman and the boy.

Guo Yan-zhi couldn't remain still and relaxed anymore. He sat up feeling very unpleasant.

A new image immediately appeared on the screen.
A young man was in a large wardrobe with its door closed. That was Guo Yan-zhi's father, a teen-ager. Outside the closet stood the young man's mother, or Guo Yan-zhi's grandma. Holding a glass of water and a steamed bun, she gently knocked on the wardrobe.

"You must be hungry by now. I bring you a steamed bun and some water here. Open the door and take the food inside to eat," the woman said.

「不要打小孩子，他説沒有偷就是沒有偷！」在旁邊鼓起勇氣勸架的是年輕的祖母。

「不是他偷的，就是妳偷的！連妳一起修理！」喝醉了的祖父表情很猙獰。

畫面在棍子的起落裡消失，女人的慘叫、孩子的哭嚎聲也慢慢隱沒。

郭彥志坐不住了，他難過得坐起身子。心裡很不舒服。

緊接著出現的薄幕上有一個窩在大衣櫃裡的少年，是大概十來歲左右的爸爸。年輕的祖母站在櫃子外面，地上放著一杯水跟一個包子，她輕敲著櫃子。

「你大概肚子餓了吧！媽媽拿了個包子跟開水過來，你開門、拿進去吃。」

"I'm not hungry, and I don't want to eat. Hurry away. It will be a disaster if Dad sees you here."

"Take the food. You've locked in the closet a whole night. You must eat."

"That's all right. When Dad wakes up, he'll remember to let me out."

The young man softly stroked the raw wounds on his body, tears rolling down his cheeks, silently. He was careful not to let his mother hear or sense that he was hurting. His mother leaned on the closet feebly. It pained her to think of the wounds on her son. Tears rolled down her face, quietly.

The screen went blank.
Just then Guo Yan-zhi thought of the slap on his own face from his father. He felt gloomy. Like him, his father was a helpless, young victim of domestic violence.

Yet another new image came on the screen.
Guo Yan-zhi's parents, then in their 20s, hand in hand, were sauntering on a beach.

「我不餓，不想吃。你趕快走開，不然被爸看到了就慘了！」

「你拿進去吃！關在衣櫃裡已經一個晚上了！不吃不喝怎麼行？」

「沒關係！等爸酒醒了，就會記得讓我出來！」

在衣櫃裡的少年輕撫著身上的累累傷痕，偷偷落淚，但小心地沒讓母親聽到。櫃子外頭的母親軟弱地靠在櫃子上，心疼孩子身上的痛，臉上的淚水也沒有停止。

第二個畫面逐漸變成空白。郭彥志忽然想起爸爸的那一巴掌，心情開始沉重。原來爸爸曾經也是個被家暴迫害的無助孩子。

第三個畫面是二十多歲的爸爸跟媽媽，兩個人牽著手在海邊漫步。

His father rounded up all of his determination that he could find, took a deep breath, and came clean with her on everything about his past.

"My father believed that the more severely he beat up his child, the more the child would go places. On top of that, he was alcoholic and addicted to gambling, so consequently my mother and I had really taken a bad beating from him over the years," Guo Yan-zhi's father said.

"But don't you worry about that. I guarantee that I'll never behave like my father."

He continued, "I'll step out of the horrible shadow of his alcoholism and gambling addiction. I'll be free of his bad influence. I am sure that I can forget all those nightmares and start a happy family with you."

Holding his hands, Guo Yan-zhi's mother said bravely and confidently, "I believe you."

His father looked clear-headed and clear-eyed, but Guo Yan-zhi was desperate, yelling loudly, "No! You haven't done as you promised. You haven't!"

爸爸鼓起勇氣，告訴媽媽自己的過去。

「我父親相信棍棒打得越兇、孩子就會越有出息。再加上他愛喝酒又愛賭博，我跟我母親常常都被修理得很慘。」

「妳不要擔心，我保證絕對不會跟我父親一樣！」

「我會走出酗酒愛賭的父親跟他的暴力陰影，一定不會被影響！」
「我一定可以忘掉那些噩夢！建立一個幸福的家庭。」

媽媽很堅定地握著爸爸的手，語氣充滿信任。
「我相信你！」

郭彥志看著薄幕上眼神清澈的爸爸，失望地大喊：「不！你答應了，但你沒做到！你沒有！」

Suddenly, Green Fairy appeared in the boat, sitting across from Guo Yan-zhi.

She sighed slightly and said slowly, "Your father did try to control himself, but it's a shame that he lost control during a stretch of the time. Frustration from work and self-pity of his own childhood were like layers of pain that were woven into a cocoon, trapping him inside from which he was unable to get out. And the worst part was he had chosen alcoholism and drug addiction to avoid facing reality, thus repeating the tragedy."

GF continued, "Did you know that he has regretted that he had accidentally slapped your face the other day?"

"Yeah right. He hasn't told me," Guo Yan-zhi said coolly.

"See for yourself," Green Fairy said and waved her hand to summon a wide screen.

First off it showed the bedroom of Guo Yan-zhi's parents after his father had slapped him on the face. The door was tightly closed, his father kneeling on the floor apologizing and his mother sobbing nonstop.

小船上突然多了一個人，坐在郭彥志對面的是小綠。

小綠輕輕嘆了一口氣，緩緩地說著：「你的爸爸試著想要克制自己。可惜，他有段時間無法控制。因為工作的挫折與童年引起的自憐，一層一層的苦痛織成了繭，困住了他而走不出來，然後最糟糕的是：他選擇了用酒跟賭逃避，重蹈了悲劇。」

「其實，你爸爸不小心打了你一巴掌的那天晚上，他非常懊悔。」

「是嗎？他沒跟我說！」郭彥志表情很冷漠。

「你自己看吧。」小綠手一揮舞。面前又出現一個寬幅的薄幕。

畫面上出現了那天晚上關緊房門的主臥室裡，跪著道歉的爸爸，和不停哭著的媽媽。

"I'm sorry. I'm sorry. I don't know why I've become a carbon copy of my father," his father said.

"You promised and you guaranteed," said his mother.

"I don't want to be like certain people in this world, and my father is on the top of that list," Guo Yan-zhi's father said. "But these nightmares have haunted me nonstop...I can't run away from them."

"You are not to hurt Yan-zhi; that's my bottom line and you know it," his mother said.

"I beg you to give me one more chance. Forgive me," his father said.

"No, let me beg you to quit drinking and quit gambling, okay? Will you agree to a divorce?" his mother asked.

His father said nothing in response.

She continued, "Please give Yan-zhi and me a chance. When you have succeeded in quitting drinking and gambling, come back to us. Allow Yan-zhi a chance to have a better father, and allow me to have a better you as a husband, okay?"

「對不起，對不起，我不知道我為什麼變成了我父親的翻版。」

「你答應過的，你保證過的。」

「這個世界上我最不想的就是跟我父親一樣，可是那些噩夢一直糾纏我，我沒辦法！我逃不出去……」

「你知道那是我的最後底線，你不能傷害彥志。」

「求求妳，再給我一次機會好不好？原諒我……」

「是我求你。你去戒酒、戒賭好不好？你答應離婚好不好？」

「……」

「求你給我們母子一個機會，讓彥志能重新有一個好爸爸，讓我重新跟一個更好的你在一起，好不好？」

"Okay! For you, for Yan-zhi, and for our future, I agree to divorce," Yan-zhi's father replied.

Guo Yan-zhi' father had just made a very difficult decision to divorce. He was hurting.

"Quitting drinking and gambling will be very tough, but I'll work very hard at that," his father said with resolve and courage.Mom gave her hand to Dad to pull him up. The two of them embraced and cried.
The screen gradually disappeared.

Guo Yan-zhi had thought at first that he had done something wrong that had made them to divorce. He was quite surprised to find out that Mom had asked for a divorce to help Dad get rid of his bad habits and that Dad had agreed to a divorce so that he could quit his own bad habits and make his whole family happy.

"Your father have worked very hard at his goals these days," Green Fairy. "He has already quit gambling altogether. Good for him." GF continued with a little sorrow in her tone.

「好！為了妳、為了彥志、為了我們的未來……我同意
離婚！」

爸爸很困難地同意了媽媽提出的離婚。他的表情十分痛
苦，但語氣裡有堅決與勇氣。

「要戒酒戒賭不是件容易的事，但我會非常努力。」媽
媽用力把爸爸扶了起來，兩個人抱著頭哭了。
薄幕上的畫面也漸漸消失。

郭彥志原本擔心是自己做錯了什麼，才讓爸媽選擇離
婚。沒想到，媽媽是為了讓爸爸改過向善、洗心革面重
新做人，而要求離婚；而爸爸是為了讓一家人幸福，痛
下決心改變自己、戒掉惡習，而同意離婚。

「你爸爸這段時間非常努力，他已經戒掉了賭這個惡
習，很不容易。」小綠眼神裡有讚賞，但接下來語調帶
點遺憾。

"In fact, he has almost quit drinking, but, because he had previously drunk too much, he has suffered from alcoholic hepatitis."

"Now, what kind of a person do you think your father is? Is he still a beast?" Green Fairy gently asked Guo Yan-zhi.

Tears, held back for some time, now gushed down Guo Yan-zhi's face. He no longer held a grudge against the slap on his face. He sympathized with his father for having such a tough childhood, and he admired him for his courage and determination to rid himself of bad habits and change his own destiny.

"Dad has been like a child, allowing himself to be shackled in that dark wardrobe in his mind until recently. Now he's trying to free himself from that," Guo Yan-zhi said, his clenched fist now relaxed. "I'll not allow myself to get entangled in a grudge against a slap. Instead, I'll let that pass so I can move on."

"Your determination has added wings to this small boat," Green Fairy said. A sail had just grown back to the boat. With the sail raised, the boat sped ahead.

「酒也戒得差不多了。可惜他之前喝了太多酒，酒精性肝炎，所以肝臟不太好。」

「你現在，覺得爸爸是個怎樣的人？還是怪獸嗎？」小綠溫柔地看著郭彥志。

郭彥志忍了半天的眼淚終於滴落了下來，他不再記恨爸爸的那一巴掌。他同情爸爸的過去，也佩服爸爸戒掉惡習改變命運的勇氣與決心。

「爸爸像個小孩，困在那個黑暗的櫃子裡，很久很久之後才有辦法離開。」郭彥志握拳後鬆開。「我不會讓自己糾結在一個巴掌裡，我會面對跟放下。」

「你的決心讓小船有了翅膀。」小綠微笑地看著小船再度變身長出風帆，揚帆而動的船速度很快。

Now the blue light had all disappeared and Guo Yan-zhi found himself back in his own room.

"What are you going to do next?" Green Fairy asked though she knew what the answer would be.

"I want to draw a card with a small sailboat in the sea, trying to ride the wind and waves."
"I want to cheer for my dad and tell him that he can successfully stop drinking and gambling. He is really a superhero in my mind!"
"And I wish him a speedy recovery. Mom and I are waiting for him. Without him, our family can't possibly be sweet."

"GF, thank you for leading me to discover my dad," Guo Yan-zhi said seriously.

"I cheer for you. You can still make it in time for the evening visit," Green Fairy said as her image began to blur. "Remember what the incense stick tells you."

轉眼間藍光已全部消失，郭彥志發現自己回到那個原本有點平凡的房間。

「等一下你打算做什麼？」小綠有點明知故問。

「我要畫一張小卡片，畫一條大海中的小帆船，努力乘風破浪的故事。」
「我要幫爸爸加油打氣。告訴爸爸，他能成功戒酒戒賭，真的是我心目中的超級英雄！」
「還有，我希望也祝福爸爸早日康復，我跟媽媽等著他，甜蜜的家庭不能少了爸爸。」

「小綠，謝謝你。讓我重新認識我爸爸！」郭彥志的表情很認真。

「加油！你可以趕得及晚上的探病時間。」小綠身形開始模糊。
「天香告訴你的話，要記住喔。」

Guo Yan-zhi took out a blank card and a watercolor paint set as he looked at the incense stick, which had thoroughly burned up by now. A message had emerged on top of the ashes: Steering.

The cheerful, smiling, and music-like voice of Green Fairy came through. "In your mind, your dad is a grownup in a child's skin, and in my mind, you are a mature adult who takes on the shape of a child. Guo Yan-zhi, one day you'll be a superior helmsman who never goes astray in the journey of life, wherever you are or whatever heaven may throw your way."

郭彥志一邊拿出水彩跟卡紙，一邊看向天香。天香燒完的灰燼裡出現兩個字：掌舵。

小綠帶著笑意的聲音像樂音一般悅耳；「在你心中，爸爸是個會犯錯而長不大的小孩；在我眼裡，你可是個小孩樣的成熟大人呢！郭彥志，有一天，你會成為最優秀的舵手，不管在哪裡、遇到什麼事，永遠都不會迷失正確的方向。」

第七個任務
Mission Seven

真正的友情
Vanity and friendship

Xu Jia-qi went to a gift shop after school. Standing in front of the store, she felt lousy as she pondered whether to go in. It would be Xiao-fang's birthday tomorrow, so if she didn't buy a present now, it would be too late. One problem was that she had little money for a discretionary purchase like this. Another problem was whatever she bought would not likely be good enough in Xiao-fang's eyes. In a class gathering last week, Xu Jia-qi, like everyone else in her class, put a secret present in the pile for drawing. She had wrapped a piece of beautiful paper around a notebook, the very best one in her possession, the one that she had cherished too much to use.

Xiao-fang drew the notebook, but she wasn't impressed. She apparently was disgusted by what she had chosen.
"I've waited for this secret present for a long time, but see what I've drawn!" Xiao-fang grunted. "The wrapping was beautiful, so I thought it must be a gem inside."

"I already have several notebooks like this one at home, all unused," Xiao-fang continued.

"Indeed. Who gave this mindless present? Give me a break," another classmate added.

放學後，許佳綺悶悶不樂地站在禮品店的門口，猶豫著要不要走進店裡。明天就是同學小芳的生日，再不買禮物就來不及了；可是自己的口袋不深，零用錢很少。上個禮拜班級同樂會舉辦抽獎活動，每個人都要提供禮物，她交出了一本包裝得很美麗的筆記簿，那是連自己都捨不得用的漂亮本子，可是抽中禮物的小芳卻一臉嫌棄。

「真是！害我期待這麼久！包裝這麼用心，我還以為是什麼珍寶呢！」

「這種本子我家裡有好幾本，放在那邊都還沒有用！」

「就是說嘛！這禮物是誰準備的？也太沒誠意了！」

"Take it if you want it. No big deal," Xiao-fang said.

As her classmates discussed this and other presents, Xu Jia-qi just listened quietly, showing no emotions even though she had been badly hurt by what's being said about the present she had brought. They didn't know who had contributed that notebook. But Cunyan knew because she had collected presents from all kids. Cunyan gave Xu Jia-qi a side-glance to gauge her reaction to those unflattering remarks. Xu Jia-qi was too upset to notice Cunyan.

"Tomorrow is Xiao-fang's B'day. Don't lose face again," Cunyan whispered to Wu Jia-qi knowingly.

Xu Jia-qi thought to herself, "Xiao-fang is so popular that she's sure to receive lots of presents. My gift must be presentable." This morning Xu Jia-qi had asked her grandpa for extra spending money. Grandpa wanted to know why….

"What for? Didn't I just give you some allowance? Are you paying some fees at school?"

「你要的話，送你！我才不稀罕！」

那天，許佳綺聽著同學們七嘴八舌的議論，默默在一旁不敢有任何表情，但是心裡很受傷。負責跟同學收摸彩禮物的春燕，瞇起眼睛，偷偷地研究著許佳綺的表情，但許佳綺並沒有發現。

「明天小芳生日，不能再丟臉了。」

許佳綺心想：小芳的人緣很好，收到的禮物一定也很多，不能漏氣。
今天早上出門前，為了多要一點零用錢，跟阿公差點吵起來。阿公很囉唆，一直問東問西。

「妳要這個錢要做什麼？零用錢不是才剛給妳？是學校要繳什麼錢嗎？」

"No. Grandpa, I want to buy a gift for a friend."

"What! So much money for a gift to a friend?"

"Other kids give really expensive stuff, Grandpa," Xu Jia-qi said. "If I don't give anything or give some cheap things, I'm going to lose face."

"A real friend doesn't mind how little money a present may cost. Sincerity is more important," Grandpa said.

"Grandpa, just leave me alone. I've fallen behind other kids in my class in many other ways. That's bad enough, so I can't also lose on this gift giving front!" Xu Jia-qi said, but that's only part of what's really bugging her. She bit her lips and choked back the rest of it just in the nick of time, which would have been, "The parents of all my classmates are very young, but my guardian is my old and poor grandfather. I feel that I've lost face big time." Xu Jia-qi thought better of that. After all, it didn't seem an opportune time for such a conversation when she was asking Grandpa for extra money.

「不是啦！阿公，你不要管那麼多，我要買東西送我朋友。」

「買東西送朋友？需要花這麼多錢嗎？」

「阿公，人家都送很貴的禮物，只有我沒送或送太便宜的東西，會很丟臉！」

「是朋友的話，不會計較禮物是多少錢買的。心意比較重要。」

「阿公，你不要管啦！在班上我什麼都輸別人很多，已經很糟糕了！」
許住綺差一點衝口而出，別的同學的爸爸媽媽都很年輕，只有自己的家長是又老又窮的阿公，真的很沒面子。但在跟阿公多要點零用錢的時候，抱怨這個好像不太好。

"Please, Grandpa. I really can't lose any more face."

Grandpa slowly turned around to take out a metal box from under the table. He took out a hundred-dollar bill, a 50-dollar and a few 10-dollar coins. When he was about to start picking out 1-dollar coins, Xu Jia-qi cut in, "Don't worry about the ones. Coins are very heavy."
She stuffed the money into her pocket and hurried out to school.

It's not that she didn't appreciate Grandpa; she really appreciated him. Without Grandpa, Xu Jia-qi would not have a home, and she couldn't imagine where or what a homeless little girl like herself might end up.

But, appreciation aside, Grandpa was just way too old if you looked at the parents of her classmates: one staggering, gray-haired, wrinkled, senile, infirm man on the one hand and smartly-dressed parents with very eye-catching titles on their business cards on the other hand. Even those mothers who did not work outside their homes dressed and looked quite presentable, to say nothing of those who worked for pay. Against this backdrop, Xu Jia-qi's grandpa was a scavenger—in rags and filthy—always struggling to squeeze out a living for the two of them.

「拜託啦！阿公，我真的不能再丟臉了！」

阿公慢吞吞地轉身，拿出放在桌子下面的鐵盒，打開後，緩緩拿出一張皺巴巴的百元鈔票，數著一個五十元和幾個拾元銅板，正要數一塊錢銅板的時候，許佳綺開始不耐煩。

「一塊錢就不用了！帶一大堆零錢在身上很重！」許佳綺連忙把阿公拿出來的錢放進口袋，趕著出門上學。

她不是不感謝阿公的撫養與照顧；從小就沒有看過爸爸媽媽，如果沒有阿公，自己還真不知道會在哪裡流浪，連個家也沒有。

但是，跟同學的家長比起來，阿公真的太老了！行動蹣跚不說，滿頭白髮加上臉上布滿皺紋。同學們的爸爸工作都很稱頭，名片拿出來頭銜很亮眼；她們的媽媽就算是家庭主婦也很注重打扮，更不用提媽媽是職業婦女的了。只有自己的阿公，靠撿垃圾賣破爛維生，衣服總是舊舊髒髒的窮酸樣。

Xu Jia-qi couldn't help feeling inferior, inadequate, and angry every time she thought of her grandpa and their lot. She had always suspected that her classmates—fully aware that she was in a skip-generation family and the destitute of her family—had behind her back made fun of her. She felt that a lack of funds to buy presents for her classmates had led them to ostracize her. Yes, they had blackballed her. She didn't feel that she belonged in their circle.

"It's all Grandpa's fault; he made me lose face," she complained to herself before coming back to reality. She took a deep breath and went into the gift shop.

After looking over and weighing again and again the things that the store had to offer, Xu Jia-qi settled on a small purse for keeping change money, the one with the image of a little kitten. Though the least costly thing in the whole store, it still cost Xu Jia-qi a lot of money.

"I've never had enough money," murmured Xu Jia-qi.

Just then, she remembered what Cunyan had whispered to her during recess: "Jia-qi, need money? Want to make some money?"

每次想到阿公，許佳綺總覺得自卑又生氣。她疑心同學們排擠自己、背後偷偷嘲笑，就是因為知道自己是隔代教養，是被阿公養大的。因為沒辦法要到足夠的錢請客送禮物，所以才無法跟大家融在一起。

「都是阿公害的！害我沒面子！」

許佳綺在店裡看來看去，最後挑了一個裝零錢的貓咪小錢包，那已經是店裡最便宜的東西，但還是很貴。

「錢到用時方恨少！永遠不夠用！」

許佳綺邊碎唸邊想起，下課時同學春燕偷偷拉她到校園角落說的話。
「佳綺，妳缺不缺錢？想不想賺錢？」

Xu Jia-qi had replied, "It's not easy to make money."

"But it is for me and Laige. Hear me out," Cunyan said. "Laige works at a nightclub. He's well-connected. He has some little good things that he needs people to sell on campus. Anyone who sells those things makes easy money," Cunyan said.

"How to sell that stuff? What's that stuff?" Xu Jia-qi asked.

"Just some little things that make people high, like coffee, tea, and snacks that are very cheap, eye-catching, and very easy to sell," Cunyan couldn't stop talking.

"What are those? Drugs?" Xu Jia-qi felt uneasy.

"Nay, they're the in-thing, not drugs," Cunyan said. "Even police couldn't find signs of drugs in the urine tests that they had conducted."

Cunyan looked around to make sure that nobody was around before taking some nicely-packaged things from her pocket. Those really looked just like ordinary jelly, plum powder, chocolate bars, and candy.

「要賺錢，沒那麼容易吧……」

「我在夜店認識一個很有辦法的大哥，我們都叫他賴哥，他有一些有意思的好東西，要找人在校園幫忙推廣宣傳一下。賣那些的話，輕輕鬆鬆就可以賺錢。」

「要怎麼推廣宣傳？是賣什麼東西？」

「就是一些會 high 的咖啡、茶和零食……，很便宜、包裝也很好看，很好賣！」

「那是什麼？不是毒品吧？」

「沒啦！那是流行，不是吸毒啦！我跟妳講，連警察驗尿都驗不出來的啦。」

春燕張望了一下，確定周圍沒有人後，偷偷從口袋拿出幾個外觀很小巧的零食，外包裝就跟一般的果凍、梅子粉、巧克力、糖果一樣。

"Won't you say that these new things look ordinary? Nobody will find out," Cunyan assured Xu Jia-qi. "There's even beverages, like ready-to-drink coffee, mile tea, and juice. If you are interested, I'll show you later."

"Think about it, OK?" Cunyan pressed on. "I've heard that your grandfather has raised you, so you probably feel that you don't have enough spending money."

"Let me think it over," Xu Jia-qi said hesitantly.

"You have one night for that. This golden window of opportunity will remain open to you till tomorrow. Then it will be closed forever," Cunyan said.

"Isn't tomorrow Xiao-fang's birthday?" Xu Jia-qi asked.

"Of course it is. How else can I afford to buy expensive presents? One must know how to make good money, you understand? BTW, you aren't going to tell on me, are you?" Cunyan said, seemingly on her guard.

「妳看，這種新型的看起來很正常吧！不會被發現的！我跟妳講，還有飲料型的，有咖啡包、奶茶包、果汁，妳有興趣的話，改天我再拿給妳看！」

「妳考慮考慮，我聽說妳是阿公養大的，零用錢應該不是很夠用。」

「我想一下。」許佳綺有點遲疑。

「就讓妳考慮一個晚上！好機會只到明天，錯過就沒了！」

「明天不是小芳生日？」

「對呀！妳以為我怎麼會買得起很貴的禮物？要懂方法賺錢才會有錢呀！對了！妳不會出賣我吧？」春燕的眼神笑意中帶點防備。

"No, I will not. You're my friend," Xu Jia-qi assured her.

"I only tell you about this opportunity because you are not just any friend, but the best friend. Remember, you must decide by tomorrow. If you want in on the action, I can even give you a few free trial packs. That's what a good friend does."

"But I'm not good at selling, not at all...," Xu Jia-qi said, still unsure.

"It's a snap. No sweat. If you become my downline, I will teach techniques to sell those things. Just learn from me. I'll be waiting for your decision. We'll wait for you to join us."

Standing outside the store, Xu Jia-qi thought: Cunyan, always forthright, is one of the very few in class who are nice to me. If I agree to join her, my purse will be full of money; I'll turn eyes; I can buy anything I want, treat people and shower them with gifts; just imagine how many friends I can make...

"It won't be a bad idea to give it a try. It's free, anyway. A good friend will do me no harm," Xu Jia-qi unknowingly said out loud.

「不會！妳是我的朋友！」

「不只是朋友，還是好朋友才會跟妳講。記住，期限是明天！妳答應的話，還可以讓妳免費先試用幾次，夠意思吧！」

「可是我不太會賣東西…」

「簡單啦！如果妳當我下線，以後我再教妳賣那些東西的技巧，妳跟我學就好！我等妳喔！等妳加入我們！」

站在店門口的許佳綺想著，春燕一向很豪爽，是班上少數對自己態度還不錯的同學。如果答應了她，以後就可以荷包滿滿、走路有風，想買什麼都沒問題；也可以常常請客送東西，就會交到更多的朋友。

「試試看也不錯，反正免費！好朋友不會害我的！」許佳綺不知不覺大聲說了出來。

"Are you quite sure that she's a good friend?" a bookish woman walked out of the store and asked, a little annoyed in her tone. "Xu Jia-qi, have you thought it through?"

"Who are you? Do I know you?" Xu Jia-qi said nervously. She wondered whether this woman was a well-informed plain clothes police woman. Could they really be so omnipresent that they have begun to tail me before I even join Cunyan?

"I'm Green Fairy. Just call me GF. Make sure you use this present tonight," GF said a little emotionally as she carefully handed a cloth bag to Xu Jia-qi, a bag that appeared to be a cut above the small purse for change money that she had just bought in the store.

"How much is it?" Xu Jia-qi said. She's reluctant to buy another thing as she had just a few coins left in her pocket.

"Priceless," GF said seriously.

"Impossible. There's a price tag on everything, whether it's family love, friendship, or presents. You pay for everything," Xu Jia-qi frowned and shook her head.

「妳真的確定，她是妳的好朋友？」短髮書卷氣的女生從店裡走出來，語氣有點怒意，看著許佳綺。「許佳綺，妳真的考慮清楚了嗎？」

「妳是誰？妳認識我嗎？」許佳綺有點緊張，該不會是什麼消息靈通的便衣女警吧？難道自己都還沒有加入，就被跟蹤盯上了嗎？

「我是小綠，這個禮物請妳今晚一定要用！」小綠有點壓抑情緒，慎重地交給許佳綺一樣東西，一個看起來比剛剛店裡買的小錢包更有質感的布包。

「多少錢？」許佳綺有點遲疑，口袋裡的銅板剩下不多。

「無價！」小綠認真的説。

「怎麼可能？什麼東西都有價位的，親情是、友情是、禮物也是，都要付出代價的。」許佳綺皺眉搖頭。

"What makes anything precious is not its price, but its pricelessness. Family love, friendship, and this present from heaven are priceless," Green Fairy insisted. "For something, you pay a price far dearer than you can imagine, for others you get a value far more precious than you know."

Xu Jia-qi went home. Before going to bed, she put the present for Xiao-fang in her book bag. Then she stared at the cloth bag that Green Fairy had given her. A gift from heaven? Sounds more like an odd thing emerging onto the world stage. Could Green Fairy be a competitor of Laige and Cunyan? Green Fairy looked quite intellectual, righteous, and connotative, so she didn't seem malicious. With that, Xu Jia-qi carefully opened the cloth bag.

Following Green Fairy's directions, she lit the incense stick. As smoke rose, green light began to flow and spread out from the veins of the divine leaf, the surface of which began to expand unceasingly into a broad plain where breezes gently blew.
Xu Jia-qi looked down only to find herself walking on a large swath of grassland, which, though slightly hilly, seemed to extend to the end of the horizon. She could not help wandering with the flickering green light. Fresh, grassy scents abounded in the air, making her feel bright and cheerful.

「真正貴重的是價值不是價格。親情是、友情是、天界的禮物更是。」小綠眼神清澈、態度很堅持。「有的代價，遠比妳知道的還要高；有的價值，比妳想像的還要貴重。」

回到家，睡覺前，許佳綺把明天準備要送小芳的禮物收進書包裡，然後看著書包裡那個陌生的布包發呆。她心中很疑惑，天界的禮物？聽起來也很像是什麼新興的怪東西。該不會是賴哥跟春燕的同行吧？不過，小綠看起來很知性、很正氣、很有內涵，應該沒有惡意才對。許佳綺小心翼翼地打開了布包。

她照著小綠的叮嚀點燃了天香，當天香閃著火星冒煙時，葉子的葉脈竄動著草綠色的流光，葉子的表面開始放大再放大、變得越來越寬廣遼闊。陣陣清風徐徐吹著，許佳綺低頭一看，發現自己居然走在一大片草原上，雖然有些許高低起伏，可是遠遠看去沒有邊際。她不自覺地跟著忽隱忽現的綠色亮點漫步。一股清新的青草味道撲鼻而來，整個人心情都很舒適開朗。

She looked leisurely at the distant sky. People were flying kites, which swayed this way and that with the wind. That was a beautiful scene. Just then a kite flew near and stopped right before her. A video screen on the kite was showing colorful images and sounds.

Xu Jia-qi checked out the screen and saw Cunyan, her classmate, dressed beautifully and whispering to a rebellious-looking man in a nightclub. That man was Laige, the man behind the business opportunity that Cunyan had told Xu Jia-qi about. The Western pop music all around was very loud and strong. Xu had to pay careful attention in order to clearly make out what Cunyan and Laige were saying.

"You said you were recruiting a downline. What's her name again?" Laige said.
"Xu Jia-qi, my classmate," Cunyan said.
"Is she reliable?"

"She and her grandfather live alone, and she needs money really bad," Cunyan replied. "I've observed her for a while. She's easygoing, has no opinion of her own, and she believes whatever I tell her. Laige, you must trust me on this one."

她悠閒地看著遠方，好像有人正在放風箏；迎風搖曳，非常美麗。就在這個時候，一個風箏朝自己飛來，就停在眼前，風箏上面閃動著彩色的聲光與畫面。

猛一看，同學春燕打扮十分俏麗，正在夜店跟一個外表很叛逆不羈的男人交頭接耳。四周西洋流行音樂的樂聲節拍非常強烈。春燕跟賴哥的對話聲要很仔細聽才能聽得清楚。

「妳說妳準備找的下線叫什麼名字？」
「許佳綺。我的同班同學。」
「她可靠嗎？沒問題吧？」

「她家只有她跟阿公兩個人，很缺零用錢。我注意她一陣子了，她很好說話，沒什麼主見，跟她說什麼、她就信什麼。」春燕有點撒嬌。「賴哥，你要相信我的眼光。」

"You can sweet talk and persuade anyone into believing anything you say. You're good at coaxing people. The prey you have spotted can't escape," Laige smiled.

"That's true, but I've learned all this from you," Cunyan said wryly. "You've been a great teacher, Laige."

"Just use the talking points we have, like you're her good friend, and as such, you wanted to share the good stuff with her. Our products are packaged for easy handling and acceptance. Free trials and easy money will surely persuade her," Laige said excitedly, his saliva shooting out. "It's so embarrassingly easy to make quick bucks selling emerging drugs on campuses."

"Xu Jia-qi is very worried that she may be blackballed by other kids, that she will not have friends because she has no money, so I'm sure she will join us," Cunyan said. "Find a few more downlines like her, then our business can thrive and mushroom like a pyramid scheme or direct selling."

「妳呀！妳這個人嘴巴甜、很會說話，很會哄人，被妳看準的獵物跑不掉的啦。」賴哥嘻皮笑臉。

「哪是啊，我都是跟賴哥你學的。」春燕的臉在夜店的光影裡顯得有點狡詐。「是你教得好嘛！」

「就用當好友、分享好東西這套話術；我們的產品包裝得很平易近人；加上免費試用，賺錢容易；一定可以成功說服的。」賴哥口沫橫飛，十分得意。「校園要推銷販賣新興毒品簡直輕鬆賺，太容易了！」

「許佳綺很怕被排擠，很怕沒錢沒朋友，所以一定會點頭答應的。多找幾個這樣的下線，我們的生意就會跟老鼠會、直銷一樣，可以越做越大。」

"What pyramid scheme! That's an ugly name," Laige said as he took out a pack of beautifully wrapped chocolate candy bars. "We allow those poor kids whom nobody cares about to sell for you and me so we can keep getting the latest and greatest gear and gadget. Make no mistake. It's a big business."

The kite shook for a while and was blown away by the wind.

Xu Jia-qi, shocked, fixated on the disappearing kite, unsure what to make of it. But before she could feel sorry for herself, the second kite appeared in front of her.

On the screen, a girl was sitting on a toilet; she had been sitting there all day long. The girl appeared to be at a loss: a very thin face with sores, slightly sunken cheeks, dark circles around the eyes, and an ashen complexion.

She didn't appear to be focusing on anything particular in her gaze, and she murmured.

Snippets of her diary appeared on the screen with voice-overs.

「什麼老鼠會，多難聽。」賴哥打開桌上精緻包裝的特製巧克力。「我們是讓那些沒人關心的孩子，幫我們買賣追求刺激的好東西！大事業，妳懂吧！」

風箏一陣抖動，被風一吹，很快飛走了。

許佳綺愣愣地看著遠去的風箏，心裡有點煩悶。她還來不及難過，第二個風箏又飛了過來。

畫面中一個女孩坐在馬桶上，一坐就一整天。女孩茫然無神，一張臉十分消瘦、兩頰有點凹陷，臉上長了幾個毒瘡，眼眶周圍發黑，氣色很不好。

女孩兩眼視線沒有焦點，一直獨個喃喃自語說著聽不懂的話。

畫面上，女孩的日記裡散亂的文字片段出現，以一種第三者的口氣像旁白般誦唸著。

"I thought it's just a little fun, recreational, so I got doped up with my friends, to get high together."

"They threatened that if I didn't inhale with them, I would be ungregarious."

"I said to them, 'Who's scared? Not me. I'll try it.'"

"But nobody told me that ecstasy would be so short-lived and the consequence would be so severe!"

"I can remember less and less, and I'm becoming less able to talk."

"Who am I?"

When the handwriting became more and more messy and illegible, an authoritative voice suddenly cut in.

"I'm Dr. Zhang. I'm sorry to tell you that your daughter has taken ketamine, which has damaged her bladder mucosa and caused irreversible fibrosis of the bladder, which has now lost its ability to store urine."

"What will bladder fibrosis do to her?" the girl's panicky father asked in a tense voice. Her mother sobbed beside him.

「我以為只是好玩，就跟著朋友一起茫，一起享受興奮感覺。」

「他們説我不跟著一起吸，就是不合群。」

「我説誰怕誰，吸就吸嘛！」

「沒有人告訴我快樂這麼短，後果這麼嚴重！」

「越來越記不起來，話也不太會講了！」

「我是誰？」

當字跡越來越凌亂到難以辨認，一個權威的聲音突然插入。

「很抱歉，我是張醫師，你的女兒吸食Ｋ他命，使膀胱黏膜受損，造成不可逆的膀胱纖維化，讓膀胱喪失了儲存尿液的功能。」

「膀胱纖維化會怎麼樣？」驚惶的父親聲音很緊張。母親在一旁啜泣。

"Once the bladder has become fibrotic, the patient will be constantly accompanied by diapers and toilets," said Dr. Zhang.

"What can we do? What can we do? She's so young...," the parents cried out helplessly.

All the while, the girl just stared into the air without any expression of emotions.

The kite, and the girl's cadaverous face, slowly drifted away in the wind.

A familiar figure appeared on the lawn, walking toward Xu Jia-qi. "Only a wise person can halt it when there's still time," Green Fairy said.

"But I need friends. I'm too lonely," Xu Jia-qi said, her head hung low, not at all sure of herself.

"What makes friends precious is sincerity, not gifts or exchanges of favors. A clique that ostracizes you is a clique not worth joining. It's more important to find real friends," Green Fairy said solemnly.

「一旦膀胱纖維化後，患者會時時刻刻離不開尿布與馬桶。」

「怎麼辦？那該怎麼辦？她還這麼年輕……」父母的聲音聽起來很傷心很無助。

而女孩，仍然呆呆地看向前方，臉上沒有表情。

風箏載著女孩漠然瘦削的臉，慢慢飛舞在風中，漸行漸遠。

接著，草坪出現一個熟悉的身影，朝著自己走來。
「我是小綠，在來得及的時候喊停，才是聰明的人。」

「可是，我需要朋友，我太孤單了……」許佳綺低著頭，表情很沒自信。

「交朋友貴在真心，而不是用禮物、用請客來利益交換！會排擠妳的小圈圈，不值得加入。找到真朋友才是重要的。」小綠的語氣很嚴肅。

"If you make bad friends, it's not easy to start over."

"Look carefully. There are many people around you who are worth your while to know and socialize with." GF waved a hand, and many kites appeared in the sky. On each kite was at least one enthusiastic face.

There are people who work hard and earnestly in club activities. They always work quietly for the common good. They are the first ones to come in to set things up and they are the last ones to leave after they have cleaned up and put things away.

When they see people moving heavy objects, they give a hand.

When seeing other people trip and fall, they don't laugh at them. Instead, they ask: Do you need help?

Some of them volunteer to tutor for classmates who have difficulty keeping up.
They help with chores at home so their parents can get a breather.

「如果交到壞朋友，想要重新再來，那就不是件容易的事！」

「其實用心看看，妳周圍有很多值得認識跟交往的朋友。」小綠手一揮，天上出現好多個風箏。每個風箏上都至少有一張熱情的臉。

有在社團活動裡，揮汗認真付出的人，總是默默認真努力，為了大家，最早來布置、最晚忙收拾。

有人看別人搬東西時，自動伸出援手、一起幫忙搬重物。

有人看到別人摔跤，不是在一旁哈哈大笑，而是熱心開口問：需不需要幫忙。

有人自願當小老師，熱心教導其他學習有困難的同學。
有人在家裡會主動幫忙分擔家事，體貼父母的辛勞。

Some of them help the elderly or the young cross streets. Their faces are filled with the real joy of helping others.
Some of them love to read, or plant, or keep pets. Their love is touching.

Some of them have set goals and are working hard to move themselves closer to their goals.

Some people like healthy, learning, and fulfilling leisure activities. In the library or on the sports field, they learn, recharge, or sweat to make themselves better.

Some people think they are ordinary, but they are all too happy to applaud the splendor of others.

"And you can learn to make yourself better, and then try to become the best friend of that better you," Green Fairy said warmly.

Xu Jia-qi looked up and saw herself on one of the kites overhead, smiling broadly and confidently.

有過馬路會扶助老人或小孩的雞婆同學，真誠的臉上洋
溢著助人的快樂。

有喜歡閱讀、喜歡種植、喜歡養小動物的同學，他們的
愛心讓人感動。

有立定志向、就努力朝目標前行的同學。

有人喜歡健康的、學習的、充實的各種休閒活動，在圖
書館裡、運動場上，積極讓自己流汗、充電、精進，為
了更好的自己努力。

有人覺得自己很平凡，但很樂意為別人的精采而熱情鼓
掌。

「妳也可以學習，和更好的自己成為最好的朋友。」小
綠的聲音很親切。

許佳綺抬頭一望，那一大群風箏當中，有一個風箏，那
張燦笑自信的笑臉竟是自己。

"By the way, do you know that Grandpa really loves you?" Green Fairy gently moved her arms, as if pulling a huge kite with many invisible threads. A kite came slowly showing a wrinkled face with gray hair.

Grandpa was sitting on a big rock on a hillside, looking into the distance. The ground was overgrown with weeds, appearing a bit desolate. Working with recyclables had just left oily stains and filth on his clothes.

"Don't worry. I'll take care of your granddaughter," Grandpa whispered to the sky.

"I will rear her well for as long as I live, and I'll make proper arrangements for her before I die."

"We are like brothers and best friends. I have tried hard to do what you asked me to do before you left! I've raised Jia-qi well," Grandpa continued.

"She and I have lived an ordinary life, a bit hard at times but safe and sound."

「對了，妳知道妳阿公真的很疼愛妳嗎？」小綠輕輕舞動著手臂，好像用許多無形的線拉動著一個巨大的風箏，緩緩前來的風箏裡有張滿布皺紋的臉與一頭白髮。

是阿公坐在山坡的大石塊上，朝著遠方張望。地上野草叢生，荒煙蔓草，顯出有點蒼涼的味道。阿公身上的衣服，還留有剛整理完回收物而殘留的油漬與髒汙。

「你的孫女我幫你守護著，你放心。」

「我活著一天，就會好好扶養她、好好教導她。」
「萬一我不在了，我也會幫她做好安排。」

「我們是結拜的好兄弟，也是最好的好朋友。你走以前託我的事，我有努力辦到了！我把佳綺好好扶養長大了。」

「我們日子過得很平凡，雖然有點辛苦，但是平平安安。」

"Jia-qi is very sensible, well-behaved, and a good girl. I hope you can bless her from heaven, lead her onto the right road, steer her away from bad influences, and don't let her go astray," Grandpa said to his best friend, now in heaven.

Grandpa looked into the distance, appearing a little lonely, but his voice was calm and steady.

Xu Jia-qi was trembled by Grandpa's monologue. She had just heard that Grandpa had adopted her. Grandpa had pinched pennies every way he could so that he could give Jia-qi the best that he could, which she had always taken for granted. After all, she had always accepted him as her own grandpa, and it would be only natural for a grandpa to dote on a granddaughter.

Never in her wildest dream had she thought it possible that Grandpa was doing this—adopting and raising Jia-qi—for his best friend. How thoughtless had I been, Jia-qi thought to herself, for endlessly complaining behind Grandpa's back that he was old and poor!

「佳綺很懂事、很乖，是個好孩子。希望你在天上能好好保佑她，讓她走在正路上，千萬不要讓她交到壞朋友，也不要走偏走歪了！」

阿公看著遠方，背影有點孤寂，但是阿公的聲音卻很沉穩踏實。

許佳綺聽到這些話，開始全身顫抖發燙。她從來不知道，自己是被收養的孩子。阿公自己省吃儉用，總把最好的讓給佳綺。佳綺總覺得自己是阿公的孫女，受阿公寵愛理所當然。

沒想到，阿公居然是幫自己最好的朋友收養了自己。而自己竟然這麼不懂事，一直背後嫌棄阿公又老又窮。

"Now, do you know what a true good friend is and what true friendship is?" Green Fairy said. "Your parents died together in a car accident. Your blood grandfather was very sad. He later became very sick, but before he died, he entrusted you to his best and most trusted friend—your Grandpa, who has kept his promise well for more than ten years."

Xu Jia-qi was so emotionally stirred that she burst into tears. Oh, how much she regretted what she had done to Grandpa. Now she just wanted to go home on the double to take care of Grandpa.

Just then, on the screen, the area where Grandpa had been sitting on, began to change: the desolate, weed strewn place was now a vividly green and vibrant turf. It was beautiful and pleasing to the eye.

A gust blew all the kites out of sight.

When Xu Jia-qi opened her eyes, she found herself standing in her little room; it was still the same little, old room, but Xu Jia-qi felt really good in it. It felt like home.

「現在，妳懂得什麼是真正的好朋友，什麼才是真正的友情了嗎？妳親生的爸媽車禍意外一起往生，妳的親祖父很傷心，他在生病臨終前，把妳託給他這輩子感情最好、最信任的朋友。這個承諾，阿公堅持了十幾年。」

許佳綺激動得淚如雨下，充滿懊悔的她，只想快點回家好好孝順阿公。

那個巨大風箏裡的影像漸漸轉變，原本阿公坐的地方，除了石頭，只有蒼涼雜生的野草，但轉瞬間漸漸長出一片片鮮活翠綠又充滿生氣的草皮，看起來非常漂亮。

一陣強風吹過，所有的風箏都消失了。

睜開眼睛，許佳綺發現自己站在小房間裡；以前老是覺得自己的家又小又破，現在才知道有家的感覺，真好。

"I hate to go, but I must leave," Green Fairy said as she began to turn transparent. "Now do you understand what I meant by priceless?"

"I finally know. Thank you, GF," Xu Jia-qi said as she wiped away her tears.

"Oh, don't cry. It's not too late! Remember to check the incense stick for a message especially for you."

The incense stick had now completely burned up, and a message had emerged to the surface of the ashes: Cherish.

Green Fairy said, "Xu Jia-qi, true friendship can stand the test of time. You must feel and experience with your heart when you choose a friend. Please cherish everything you have and happiness will always be with you. Go, Xu Jia-qi."

「很捨不得，但我必須離開了。」小綠的身體開始變透明了。「妳現在知道我所説的無價了吧！」

「小綠，謝謝妳。我終於懂了！」許佳綺擦著眼淚，邊啜泣邊感謝。

「別哭！現在一切都來得及！記得看天香留給妳的文字訊息。」

燒完的天香灰燼裡出現兩個字：珍惜。

小綠溫柔的聲音十分動聽；「許佳綺，真正的友情，經得起時間的考驗。選擇朋友，是要用心感受與體會的。請珍惜妳所有的一切，幸福會一直與妳同在的。加油！」

Farewell, or is it the beginning of meeting again?

Now that Green Fairy has accomplished all of her seven assigned missions, she knew that she would need to leave before long, about which she began to have mixed feelings deep in her heart. On the one hand, she now had real feelings for this temporal world, and she felt reluctant to just leave it for good. On the other hand, she was very happy. She had helped seven young adults find solutions to their problems and directions in their lives. She had achieved something precious. She was grateful for being assigned these missions in this mundane world—initially meant as a punishment but turned out to be wonderful, purposeful challenges.

She should get going now, but leaving was easier said than done at the moment. She told herself: Just one moment longer. The seven teens were like old friends to her, and they held sway in her heart.

"I wonder how they're doing," Green Fairy thought to herself. "Hey, Ding Xiao-yu, Wang Zi-qiang, Fang Ya-ping, Xie You-qing, Wu Xin-jie, Guo Yan-zhi, and Xu Jia-qi, how are you guys doing?"

"It won't hurt to have another quick peek." She waved her hand, and the seven teenagers appeared in her palm in turn.

離別，也許是再會的開始

七個任務都已圓滿完成，小綠心裡有點百感交集。一方面對於人間產生了感情，知道自己離去的時間馬上就要來臨，開始變得捨不得。一方面又很開心，自己幫助了七個孩子找到問題的真相與人生的方向，她非常有成就感。更感謝自己有機會下凡到人間，將功贖罪完成這麼有意義的挑戰。

她應該要準備離開了，可是遲遲無法行動。她告訴自己：只要再一下下就好。七個孩子像七個認識很久的朋友，在心頭占了重重的分量。

「不知他們後來怎麼樣了？」

「丁曉雨、王子強、方雅蘋、謝佑青、吳欣潔、郭彥志、許佳綺，大家都好嗎？」

「就悄悄地再看一眼吧！」

她揮舞著手掌，七個孩子的影像陸陸續續在手心出現。

First off, she saw Ding Xiao-yu working in a bubble tea shop with a confident, beautiful smile on her face. Xiao-yu greeted the guests cordially and neatly. Her dexterous hands never stopping, she shook out cup after cup of delicious thirst-quenching drinks exactly as ordered. When elderly or sweaty laborers came up to order, she reminded them not to have too much added sugar.

Green Fairy believed that Ding Xiao-yu must feel quite sweet making money with her own honest labor.

Ding Xiao-yu's smiling face turned into a bundle of yellow light projecting out in all directions into the clear sky.

Far from frowning, hunched over, and glum-faced, Wang Zi-qiang had become a happier teen with more free time to do things with his friends. That change had been made possible by his frank talks with his parents. Now he could play basketball, ride bicycles, and do homework with Xu Wei and Jian Zhen-guo. He now asked his mother for permission to do house chores. His mother said, "Well, let's see. If you've done your best to prepare for your tests and you've gotten good grades, then you may help with chores."

Echoing her, his father said, "Doing chores is not a punishment but rather a reward for good behavior. Only when you've performed well enough can you be permitted to help." Wang Zi-qiang was already helping with chores as his parents tried to tease him. He was helping with cooking. Standing up straight, he appeared taller and better looking.

首先，她看到在泡沫紅茶店打工的丁曉雨，臉上的笑容踏實又美麗。曉雨親切俐落地招呼著客人，靈巧的雙手沒停過，客製化地搖出一杯又一杯好喝解渴的飲料。看到老人家或者是大汗淋漓的勞工，她還會特別關心，提醒糖可不要加得太多，適量甜對身體比較好。

　　小綠相信：對丁曉雨來說，靠自己能力實實在在賺錢的滋味，應該很甜美。

　　丁曉雨的笑臉化成一道黃光，渲染開來投射在晴朗的天空。

　　以前老是愁眉苦臉、彎腰駝背的王子強，自從跟爸媽好好溝通之後，爭取到比較多自己的自由時間，可以和徐偉和簡振國一起打球、騎腳踏車、研究功課。他也會主動要求幫忙做家事，只是媽媽總會很酷地說：「你認為你有盡力準備考試、也考得不錯的話，你就可以幫忙做家事。」

　　爸爸也會在一旁幫腔打趣：「做家事不是懲罰，是好孩子的獎勵。表現夠優秀才有資格幫忙。」幫忙做菜的王子強，腰桿挺直後，也顯得更高更清秀了。

Wang Zi-qiang turned into a bundle of indigo light projecting out in all directions into the clear sky.

Fang Ya-ping, the once social media influencer and overnight sensation wannabe, now strived to be an internationally renowned botanist. She knew well that she had a whole lot to learn, so whenever she could she worked on her English lessons, went to the library, or searched the net for plant information. She has found a worthy goal to which she could now devote all her energy pursuing.

The image of Fang Ya-ping studying a plant turned into a bunch of purple light in the shape of a beautiful arc in the sky.

Xie You-qing once had a chip on his shoulder and was always ready to get in a fist fight at the slightest provocation, but now he and his father were the best of friends. They could talk about anything openly and intimately. They wanted to make up for lost time. On holidays, they visited the childhood home of his mother and the place where his father had grown up. They went to spots where his parents had spent time dating. They sampled dishes that his parents had eaten together. All this had helped You-qing piece together snippets of his mother so now he had a clear image of his loving mother. He and his father could now cherish the memory of his mother together.

王子強的身影化成一道靛色流光，渲染開來也跟著投射在天空上。

以前超級想當網紅、要一炮而紅的方雅蘋，她現在轉念立志想當個揚名國際的植物專家。但因為認為自己還有很多地方需要加強與充實，現在一有空就專注於進修外語，平時沒事勤跑圖書館讀書或上網找植物的資料，這些成了她最熱愛的新興趣。

方雅蘋專心研究植物的模樣變幻成一道紫光，在天際形成一道美麗的弧。

以前沒事總愛握緊拳頭、好像有人找碴就準備隨時奉陪的謝佑青，現在跟爸爸就像哥兒們一般，兩人的話題很多，無所不談。兩人以前損失的相處時光，現在全都要加許多倍補回來。爸爸會帶著佑青，利用假期去探訪自己小時候成長的地方，也會帶佑青去認識媽媽的家鄉，以及分享爸爸媽媽當年約會的美景跟美味小吃。佑青藉由經歷媽媽的足跡，更能跟爸爸一起懷念那個很愛自己的媽媽。

Xie You-qing loved to smile now because he knew how much his parents loved him.

The image of Xie You-qing smiling became a band of orange light shining softly in the distant sky.

Green Fairy then saw Wu Xin-jie taking her brother and sister to her secret base. Wu Xin-jie saw the little boy again, the one who had literally smashed into her the last time, spilling his coke and staining her skirt. This time, Wu Xin-jie said to him patiently and cheerfully, "Be careful. Don't run. If you bump into other people, you may lose a coke."

The little boy was a little bit shy. He said to Wu Xin-jie politely, "Ah! Sorry, I was in too much of a hurry the last time, and I forgot to say sorry to you!"

Wu Xin-jie's siblings were very interested in her usual seat next to the big potted plants at the secret base. The two little children began to play rock paper scissors and hide and seek.

Wu Xin-jie was smiling broadly like the sun. The blush on her face turned into a bundle of red light shining warmly in the sky.

現在的謝佑青很愛微笑，因為他知道爸爸跟媽媽有多愛自己。

　　笑容滿面的謝佑青影像閃現一道橙光，柔柔地映照在天邊。

　　小綠看到吳欣潔帶著兩個年幼的弟弟妹妹，一起到她的祕密基地。當吳欣潔又遇到當初那個像火箭一樣撞過來的冒失小男孩，她很有耐性微笑叮嚀：「小心，不要跑太快，撞到人會損失一罐可樂喔！」

　　小男孩有點害羞，接著很有禮貌地對她說：「啊！不好意思，上次太急了、忘了跟妳說對不起！」

　　弟弟妹妹對大盆栽旁吳欣潔習慣的老位子很有興趣，兩個小小孩準備要猜拳玩捉迷藏。

　　吳欣潔的笑容非常陽光，臉上的一抹紅暈幻化成一道紅光，暖暖地映在天上。

Guo Yan-zhi placed the card that he had drawn under his father's pillow. On the card, the boat that tried to ride the wind and waves at a rough sea had given his father a lot of strength. Whenever the darkness of the past hit him like a nightmare, the card drawn by the son would be like a hefty and stabilizing anchor, allowing him to gather his courage and strength from his heart. He was no longer weak. Guo Yan-zhi's words, "Dad, you are my superhero," was like a super battery charger that had kept him energetic. And Guo Yan-zhi had now gotten to know his father afresh, accepted his father, and after having let go of the dark shadow of that slap, he was prepared to join his mother to welcome his father home.

Guo Yan-zhi was again lying with all of his limbs spread out, but this time he was really relaxed, sleeping in serenity. He was no longer in self-exile, no longer at a loss of motivation. He now looked forward to his father coming home healthy. It felt good to have something positive to look forward to.

The blue melancholy in Guo Yan-zhi turned into a rational and clear blue rising into the sky as a smiling blue arc.

Green Fairy was glad that she had held her tongue before chiding Xu Jia-qi for her misguided values on life and on friendship. GF was glad that she had instead chosen to take her time to guide the teen. Otherwise, her last mission could have ended up a failure.

郭彥志的卡片放在爸爸的枕頭底下，那艘海上努力乘風破浪的小船給了爸爸很大的力量。每當過去的黑暗像噩夢一般襲來，那張兒子親手畫的卡片就像一個又大又穩的錨，讓爸爸從內心滋生勇氣與力量，不再軟弱。郭彥志的那句「爸，你是我心中的超級英雄。」更是爸爸的超級電池。而郭彥志自己，重新了解爸爸、接納爸爸、放下那一巴掌的心結後，也跟著媽媽一起準備迎接全新的爸爸回家。

　　放鬆而呈大字型睡姿的郭彥志，現在單純是放輕鬆，睡臉非常平靜，不再是自我放逐、失去動力。等待爸爸康復回家的他，現在可是時刻都充滿期待與希望。

　　郭彥志身上原本藍色的憂鬱，如今變成理性而清澈的藍，在天空裡變成微笑的藍色弧線。

　　小綠回想自己差一點點控制不住情緒，想要張口責備許佳綺錯誤的價值觀與交友觀，還好忍住、選擇慢慢開導；不然最後一個任務說不定會失敗。

Xu Jia-qi was now no longer at a loss and not feeling lonely and friendless. She had now discovered that many people could be her friends, but she should choose friends carefully and sincerely. She should be choosy rather than indiscriminate. She had expressed her gratitude to her grandpa in action: sharing household chores and sorting recyclables with him.

Xu Jia-qi still liked to walk on grassland. A small blade of grass beside her quietly shifted position, rising to the horizon as a green halo.

Green Fairy raised her eyebrows and looked at the sky that now showed red, orange, yellow, green, blue, indigo, and purple arcs. She couldn't help rearranging their sequence, making them into a broad and beautiful rainbow.

Green Fairy had brought with her to this temporal world the seven tender seedlings that she had unwittingly tramped down in heaven. Each of them had in its own way helped one teenager who had sent out a cry for help. Each of them had used its own heavenly power and energy to help its charge see through his or her quandary and find a sound way out.

許佳綺現在不再茫茫然、覺得孤單沒朋友了。她發現可以當朋友的人原來有這麼多，自己應該用心好好選擇，用真心換真情。交朋友可是寧缺勿濫，更不能隨便。她對阿公的感謝也化為行動。年輕人比較有力氣，女生也能分擔家事與幫忙整理回收物。

　　許佳綺喜歡到草原上漫步的愛好依然沒變，影像裡的她，身邊的一株小草悄悄地挪了位置，移動到天邊暈染成綠色的光環。

　　小綠挑挑眉毛看著天上紅、橙、黃、綠、藍、靛、紫七色光環，忍不住動動手指，調整順序與排列之後，變成一道又寬又大美麗無比的彩虹。

　　天界的七株嫩苗，被小綠不小心得意忘形時踩壞了。小綠帶著天界七株嫩苗的葉子來到人間，幫助了人間七個發出求救訊號的孩子。這七片葉子在人間各憑本事、發揮了最大的仙力，竭盡了最大的能量；以種種不同的樣貌，帶著求救的孩子看到、聽到、想到、知道讓他們困惑的問題與找到答案。

This human world has gotten to appreciate that plants are strong, vital, and versatile. They can be used as decorations or ingredients for healing. There are also people who know how to use gardening activities as therapies to improve people's body, mind, and spirit.

Green Fairy believes that energy is indestructible and that the positive energy generated by the transformation of the seven teens will definitely resonate and energize the seven crushed seedlings in heavens to regain vitality and thrive again.

Who says the world is ruthless and dull? Far from it; the world is full of love and excitement! Green Fairy still feels it very hard to leave, but she is deeply convinced that the life wisdom that the seven teenagers have gained will sustain and flourish. She is glad that these young people—like seedlings—in the secular world have been straightened and are taking root.

Now Green Fairy is ready to go home. After crossing the Rainbow Bridge in the sky, she will be able to care for the seven seedlings in heaven again.

This farewell just may set the next meeting between Green Fairy and the seven teens in motion, and she looks forward to that.

人間也懂植物的生命力很強，植物除了觀賞、裝飾外，還能成為治療心靈的處方。還有人懂得用園藝活動來治療人，改善人的身、心、靈。

　　小綠相信能量是不滅的，這七個孩子改變時所產生的正向力量，一定也會共振，讓天界那七株被踩壞的嫩苗，感應與得到充足的生命力，重新欣欣向榮，勇猛地長成茁壯美麗的姿容。

　　誰說人間無情又落伍？人間有愛而精彩！小綠依依不捨，她深信孩子們心領神會的收穫歷久彌新。她很高興，人間的幼苗她扶正了、也發芽了。

　　現在，就等穿越彩虹七色橋之後，回天界關心那七株天界嫩苗的狀況了。這一次離別，也許，也許就是下次再會的開始。如果是，她很期待……。

已毒難回 己毀也悔

陳乃裕

一個從小家庭健全，在優渥環境中長大的孩子為什麼會接觸毒品？是朋友誘惑還是自己好奇？全部都是他的錯嗎？

父母從不能接受到最後反省，是否大人期待太多，不知不覺給孩子超負荷的壓力了？

一旦蹈入毒品的泥淖怎麼辦？那是全家的噩夢，卻也需要全家人攜手同心一起長期陪伴與抗戰。

讓我們一同看幾個真實的個案，因而了解為何「已毒難回，己毀也悔」。

個案一：讓更生人的心有個家

第一次接到警局電話，說小兒子在派出所，還以為是車禍，結果竟然因為吸毒被拘留！怎麼會？

我們都以為是孩子不學好，多年後才了解，原來大人加諸太多期盼在孩子身上，同儕間相互較量，導致承受不了壓力，想暫時逃避，在沒有戒心下被毒品攻心。

在東河服刑近兩年，做父母的每月一次帶著獄方規定的兩公斤食物，半夜兩點出門，從暗暝開車到天亮，趕在早上九點第一梯次會客。

　　獄中生活規律，孩子學會了電腦也考了照，教誨師看他眉清目秀，經常和他深談。每週親子互通書信，把看到的經書、裡面講的因緣果報，及證嚴上人的開示寫給他：一切皆因緣起，雖然身陷囹圄失去自由，但也要珍惜這一小段因緣，和人好好相處。

　　終於盼到孩子出獄了，人生重新起步。在三個多月求職過程中，雇主一開始看到履歷，與他面談都很滿意，但是當靦腆說出自己是更生人時，對方馬上變臉，請他回去等候通知，孩子的沮喪寫在臉上。剛好一位開禮儀公司的師兄急需幫手，孩子在獄中讀的佛書正好用上，也可以和喪家結善緣。

　　孩子後來去廣州工作，遇上一個好女孩，不計較他的過去，二〇一六年回臺公證結婚，婚後才知道，原來親家也是慈濟人，天賜良緣！

　　孩子感謝父母的不離不棄：「媽媽，十分感謝你和爸用愛陪伴，沒有放棄。事實上，獄友大部分很善良，本質不壞，只是沒我幸運。有些被關一整年，沒見家人來過，有的早就沒有家了，出來後大部分人再回社會，會害怕、焦慮、不適應，甚或被歧視、貼標籤，面臨現實問題，很可能反覆出入監所。其實他們在獄中學會各種職能，如果有中途之家，一定可以減少走回頭路。」

個案二：我有毒兄弟

十歲前，我住在新北市土城，父親是職業軍人，家庭堪稱和樂圓滿。後來母親罹患精神分裂症，常覺得有人要害她，所以搬離了眷村。那年她叫我去藥房買老鼠藥，我還小，買回來後出去玩，沒想到傍晚回家，母親口吐白沫，送醫已回天乏術。父親因為失去摯愛悲傷不已，以酒精麻醉自己，經常酩酊大醉，清醒的時候就去打牌。

小四的我懵懂無知，遭逢生命中的遽變，過著有一餐沒一餐的日子。念國中最好班的哥哥一直是我崇拜的英雄，這時也選擇自我放逐，成為漂丿少年。我們在國中常抽菸、翹課、喝酒、吃檳榔、打架，甚至帶武士刀壯聲勢。

我的功課一落千丈被分在放牛班，對人生充滿仇恨。曾因為抬便當與人發生爭執被毒打，因此覺得要加入幫派,因為大哥能馬上找兄弟幫我出氣,是我心目中的英雄,武力是最好的靠山。從此,我常用拳頭武裝自己,逞兇鬥狠成了生活的一部分。國中畢業後輟學,因為與人衝突,虎口被砍,縫了十一針,差點進不了軍校。唯一慶幸的是自己從沒碰毒品。

我哥哥從全校最好的班級輟學之後,加入幫派開始吸食強力膠,進出監獄算算有十三次之多。他毒癮越來越大,從強力膠、安非他命、速賜康、海洛因到大麻,也越混越大尾,帶槍討債開賭場,警察經常上門盤查。大嫂是個有內涵的女孩,也因為跟哥哥交往染上毒癮,最後毒癮難耐從八樓墜落身亡,那年才二十六歲。

一九九六年,哥哥因吸毒太深倒臥在地瞳孔放大,被送進加護病房,見到我,他眼淚奪眶而出,當下我拿出兩萬元濟助,但他早被毒魔控制了,戒毒談何容易,我在兄弟情與家庭之間痛苦擺盪著。

隔年三月,大哥出獄來要三萬元生活費,我背著太太找人借錢,甚至摘下婚戒給他典當。結果因心情不佳,又怕回去難以面對妻子,在高速公路和大客車碰撞翻覆。事後,太太沒有責備我,反而因為怕失去我而痛哭失聲,我懺悔極了。

大哥在獄中每次也說要把毒給戒了，但卻一次次失敗。他的腿斷了三次，渾身是病，我幾乎想放棄，但終究敵不過親情。

　　直到二○一二年三月一日大哥從高雄燕巢出獄，我在他床頭上放了本《靜思語》，他還幸運地找到一份收留更生人的工作。在反毒教育宣導場上現身說法，還錄製五分鐘影片，但那卻是他最後身影！半年後，房東打電話來，說他暴斃了，四十八年人生畫下句點。我心情好複雜，我沒有偏離自己的道路，終究得感謝大哥一路上以生命示現，我突然發現他是我的貴人，讓我懂得珍惜一切。衷心祝福他來生不再被毒糾纏。

個案三：毒害吾家

　　電話鈴聲劃破深夜的寂靜，那頭傳來母親淒厲的哭喊：「快回來！出事了！」二弟懸樑自盡，孱弱的母親不知哪來的力量將他抱了下來，但無論怎樣搖晃，已再也喚不醒。

　　二弟留下一封遺書：「我很後悔用到毒，我真的想改，但一次次失敗。去年阿爸也因為我的毒改不了，難過得抱憾而終，很對不起！既然改不了，決定不再拖累大家，請原諒我！」

　　毒害帶走了年僅三十歲的二弟，那是一九九二年的事。

　　我的家幸福溫馨，父親事業平順，母親生育我們五個，二弟善良熱情，是開心果，怎奈國中時跟著大弟步入吸毒之路。他們一開始吸膠、速賜康，進而安非他命，清秀的臉龐變了形，清澈的眼眸變呆滯，大弟毒癮來時還會大吼大叫，鬧得雞犬不寧，家中的金飾金條全被偷光；他也會謊騙被黑道追殺、跟朋友創業，一再騙取金錢，一再傷害父母心。

　　為了換環境，我們搬了三次家，爸媽甚至施出鐵腕，送大弟去少年觀護所，也曾帶他到苗栗、臺東、臺北晨曦會戒毒，但住不到一個月就吵著要回家，回來後又馬上買毒，輪迴不已！

　　夜路走多了，弟弟們陸續陷囹圄，對父母而言是莫大打擊，在親友間抬不起頭來，爸爸老淚縱橫：「我沒做壞失德的代誌，怎會出兩個兒子攏吸毒，用盡方法幫他們戒，攏改不起來，阮父母很痛苦，像活在地獄一般。」我也陪著掉淚。

　　二弟走了，留下厚厚一本獄中日記：「母親又寄來參仟元，自受刑至今近五年，母親每月都按時寄參仟伍仟不等，這是恆久不變的母愛！有句話說，母親對子女的愛是終身犯，不能假釋，更不能交保。今生今世欠母親的債一輩子還不清，如果這次重返社會一定要好好報答她。」「自小一直希望有個溫暖健康溫馨的家，娶妻生子，但自從染上惡習就跌入深淵，不能自拔，我絕不允許自己再蹈覆轍……，這是我最後一次入獄，往後如果再吸毒就是死期到了，自行解決，絕不苟延殘喘……」

　　一九九一年父親積勞成疾，臨終前仍放心不下弟弟們，他無力的拉著我的手：「你是老師，兩個弟弟交代給你，一定要幫他們脫離毒品。」父親抱憾而終，怎奈隔年二弟也魂斷毒海！此時大弟還在獄中，千萬封家書愛的呼喚，叮嚀他要痛改前非。這回大弟出獄後戒毒成功，成家立業了，孝順母親，熱心行善，卻罹患胰臟癌，加上之前毒品傷及內臟，他受不了去買一級毒品海洛因止痛，臨終前涕泣不止：「我看不到明天的太陽，沒機會孝順父親也來不及孝順母親，更無法看到女兒成長，只好來生報答！請幫我跟父親同葬，向他懺悔。」當時大弟四十六歲，女兒僅八歲！

　　在告別式上，長輩要以枴杖用力在棺材上敲三下，但母親不忍：「他已經改好做好子了，他沒有不孝，他是我的心肝兒！」丟下枴杖撫棺痛哭，母親喪夫又兩度喪子，情何以堪！

當時的我不願提及這段往事，至今隱隱作痛。希望人人引以為鑑，向毒品說 NO！

臺灣毒癮者約二十六萬，新生人口大多發生在十八至二十四歲，人生才要開始就被毒癮牽制，即使想戒毒，卻往往不敵心魔，導致回鍋率達七成，戒毒成功者成為相對少數，很多要靠宗教力量，強大個人意志力，或者有中途之家，以集體的包容與愛，以及相互支撐重新活過！一但陷身毒淵，要想回頭恐怕已百年身！面對毒品的誘惑，青少年朋友著實不可不慎！

七片葉子 Seven Leaves

作　　　者／涓滴水（陳穎君）
英　　　譯／湯耀洋（YY Tang）
企畫組稿／林幸惠
中文整理／胡毋意
中文校對／吳琪齡
英文校訂／張恭逢（Richard Chang）

發　行　人／王端正
總　編　輯／王志宏
叢書主編／蔡文村
叢書編輯／何祺婷
美術指導／邱宇陞
美術編輯／黃靜薇
出　版　者／經典雜誌
　　　　　　財團法人慈濟傳播人文志業基金會
地　　　址／台北市北投區立德路二號
電　　　話／（02）2898-9991
劃撥帳號／19924552
戶　　　名／經典雜誌
製版印刷／禹利電子分色有限公司
經　銷　商／聯合發行股份有限公司
地　　　址／新北市新店區寶橋路 235 巷 6 弄 6 號 2 樓
電　　　話／（02）2917-8022
出版日期／2021 年 3 月初版
定　　　價／新台幣 320 元

國家圖書館出版品預行編目 (CIP) 資料

七片葉子 = Seven Leaves/
涓滴水著；湯耀洋英譯 . -- 初版
臺北市 : 經典雜誌, 慈濟傳播人文志業基金會 , 2021.03
320 面 ; 15*21 公分
中英對照
　ISBN 978-986-99938-9-0(平裝)

　1. 青少年心理 4. 青少年成長 5. 青少年輔導 6. 青少年
問題 7. 親子關係

863.57　　　　　　　．　　　　　　110003742

小樹系列

Little Trees

小樹系列

Little Trees